Walking on Air

Also by Kelly Easton

The Life History of a Star
Margaret K. McElderry Books

Walking on Air

Kelly Easton

SAN LEANDRO
LIBRARY
HIGH SCHOOL

MARGARET K. MCELDERRY BOOKS
New York London Toronto Sydney

Margaret K. McElderry Books
An imprint of Simon & Schuster
Children's Publishing Division
1230 Avenue of the Americas, New York, New York 10020

This book is a work of fiction. Any references to historical events, real people, or real locales are used fictitiously. Other names, characters, places, and incidents are products of the author's imagination, and any resemblance to actual events or locales or persons, living or dead, is entirely coincidental.

Copyright © 2004 by Kelly Easton

All rights reserved, including the right of reproduction in whole or in part in any form.

Book design by Ann Sullivan
The text for this book is set in Hoefler Text.

Manufactured in the United States of America
2 4 6 8 10 9 7 5 3 1

Library of Congress Cataloging-in-Publication Data
Easton, Kelly.
Walking on air / Kelly Easton.—1st ed.
p. cm.
Summary: In 1931 a young girl travels around the country performing on a tightrope during revival meetings held by her father, and seeking her own answers about God, her family, and her life of poverty and homelessness.
ISBN 0-689-84875-7
[1. Family life—Fiction. 2. Clergy—Fiction. 3. Tightrope walking—Fiction. 4. Identity—Fiction. 5. Homelessness—Fiction. 6. United States—History—1919-1933—Fiction.]
I. Title.
PZ7.E13155Wal 2004
[Fic]—dc21
2002156184

FIRST
EDITION

For Isabelle Easton Spivack

Acknowledgments

For helping me stay on my tightrope, I'd like to thank the following people: Michael and Sheli Easton; Marilynn Easton; Gordon Easton; Randi Easton Wickham; Isaac Robert Easton Spivack; Joanne Baines; Nancy Antle; Shari Alvanas, of Roger Williams University; Susan Beam; Jean Brown, of Rhode Island College; Jean Brown, of Jamestown; Doriana Carella and Andrea Colognese; Kate Fillion; Bonnie Kennedy; Michaela Kennedy; Stephanie O'Neill; Patti Pereira; Pam Kosseff; Dr. Kyle Murray; and Lou Pulner. Many thanks to Arthur Jay Spivack for his support of my work, to Jane Dystel Literary Management, to Kris Williams and the other kind librarians at the Jamestown Philomenian Library.

I would also like to thank my wonderful editors at Margaret K. McElderry Books of Simon & Schuster: Emma D. Dryden, vice president and editorial director, and Sarah Nielsen.

This novel evolved from a story titled "Air" that was published in *Sojourner* magazine in 1997. The story was an honorable mention in that magazine's fiction competition, judged by Dorothy Allison.

BIBLICAL QUOTATIONS ARE TAKEN FROM THE NEW REVISED STANDARD VERSION OF THE HOLY BIBLE, PUBLISHED BY ZONDERVAN BIBLE PUBLISHERS.

FROM GOING TO AND FRO ON THE EARTH,
AND FROM WALKING UP AND DOWN ON IT.
—*The Devil speaking to God,* JOB

Another town. Wet streets and broken streetlamps. This one is not as bad as some. Only half the shops are boarded up.

We are living it up with a diner meal: white volcano of potato with lava gravy, carrots and peas, gray oblong of meat (some cow shoulder or butt).

Pa sucks on his cigarette as if it's his last. Ma raises her fork to her mouth every thirty seconds. It's like she is doing some kind of experiment and the timing has to be just right.

Occasionally, she says something pleasant, which is meant to remind Pa how nice it would be if we could all stay in one place. "Nothing like my cooking, is it?" she says, or, "Remember the roast chicken I made one Christmas when we were living in Ohio?"

As usual, Pa says nothing, just blows smoke out of his mouth as if it's words and comforting.

He rarely speaks to Ma anymore. I don't know why. Maybe he's saving his breath for when we'll haul up the tent and he will go on for hours in a voice loud and menacing enough to reach God, if He is there, and he will preach about Jesus.

I play with my food. It's another sign of my sinfulness. Pa says God is everywhere: in hungry faces, in trees, on the stripes of the barbershop pole, even in food.

God is in a mashed potato or a chunk of dead cow.

I lift my fork and set it down. I make the peas into an army of soldiers where they can triumph over the carrots.

"Eat!" Ma nags me. She's the one who should eat. Her skin is a white dress on the hanger of her bones.

"Shouldn't she keep up her strength?" she prods Pa.

Because the night hasn't gone well, Pa buttons and unbuttons his shirt cuffs, rolls up the part of his sleeve that is unraveling. Then he puts out his cigarette in his own plate of food. "Seven people," he hisses, referring to the believers who came out on this cold night to hear him preach. "Seven. You can count them on your fingers and what good'll it do ya."

Outside, the light spatter of rain turns hard. There are many hard things in the world, especially in this year of Our Lord, 1931. The world is hanging by a thread, Ma says, and the thread gets thinner and thinner. One day, it could snap.

Under the awning, I see the shadowy figure of Rhett, smoking a cigarette. He works for our family. Just once in all these years did Pa ask him to join us when we ate.

Sometimes Rhett is with us; sometimes he isn't. It's hard to figure where he goes in between. He might disappear in Kansas City and reappear in Chicago. How he keeps track of us is beyond me, but he always manages to bring me something good when he comes back: a chocolate coin, an orange, or a pencil.

As long as I remember, he has not spoken. Once I heard Ma tell someone that he had taken a vow of silence. He didn't speak up at a time when he should have, she said, and hasn't spoken since.

I think about striking up a friendship with my uneaten supper; there are days I've gone without. But before I can make a move, the waitress rushes over and sweeps my plate away.

Ma doesn't notice. She is watching the rain pour from the awning to the street, lost in an earlier time when the spirit of God made her sing, and Pa heard her voice and took her away with him. Ma thought she was marrying a man of the church. She imagined a little house, a rectory, a small garden, a choir, and works for the poor. Instead he took her *away* away: to his many and constant travels, his salvation shows for Jesus.

"Y'a were good up there on that tightrope, little girl." The waitress stands behind me. "The way you could jump and spin! I thought at any minute you would disappear into the clouds."

Sometimes I feel like my head is an apple on a pole. It feels so heavy, ready to fall and take the rest of my body with it, or just tumble off onto the floor, still talking and breathing.

I worry it could hinder my balance.

I tilt it back and look at her. Her hair is orange, her lips red.

I love strangers. What you don't know about them. What you can make them be.

"Thank you," I say.

"I'll bring ya a piece of apple pie and ice cream. On me."

"But did you see God?" Pa wraps his fingers around the waitress's wrist. The coffeepot wobbles in her hand.

"I see God everywhere. He gets in my mirror when I'm doing my face." She tugs her arm away and returns to the kitchen.

"You can see how bad it's getting. The likes of her sees God everywhere and don't think they need preaching to help them along. When people were fed and clothed"—Pa swats at an invisible fly—"Aimee Semple McPherson herself could come to town and they'd yawn and hide in their beds."

Aimee Semple McPherson is Pa's idol. She's a lady evangelist who's gotten rich and built a big temple in Los Angeles. When she preaches, crowds spill out onto the streets. Pa says she can save souls just by touching their foreheads with her little pinkie. He's even thought of renaming me after her, to remind me that I'll be a great preacher too, one day.

I can just see it. Me standing under a leaky tent in the rain, shouting scripture. Cripes!

The waitress brings my pie. The tag on her dress says GLADYS.

If I could, I would live on pie. It's as if all of the excess of feeling in these towns—the forlorn brides, the town drunks, the lonely old ladies, the hungry kids—have landed soul-flown in the crust, the weeping apples, the peaches like babies curved in their mas' bellies.

I love anything sweet: pastel candies in lines on paper strips, the flesh of pulled taffy, funnel cakes dredged in red syrup and snowy sugar, grainy cotton candy made of air.

We used to do our show in carnivals, but in these hard times, they have disappeared. Back then, when I wasn't performing, I could eat all the sweets I wanted.

I would duck into a tent with a caramel apple and see the bearded lady, the flippered man, the Siamese twins.

The Siamese twins were named Hari and Kari and they told me the story of their birth in a field of wheat. A farmer was harvesting his crop when he found them: one body, two heads. At first he thought that he had cut someone in two!

He picked up the babies. They were covered in a thin yellow fluid. He told his wife that they were probably hatched from an egg but she didn't believe him. What she believed was that he had been unfaithful and that these were his sons. God was punishing him, she thought, for his sins.

For a while she took them in. The farmer grew to love them. He loved them for their joy, the way they stuck out their two tongues and laughed when people stared at them and pointed.

My spoon slides into the pie.

"She didn't finish her supper," Ma says. "She shouldn't have dessert."

"Let her have what she wants," Pa replies. "Besides, it's free."

"Don't spill it on your costume, June," Ma adds. She sometimes thinks that I am the enemy, although I know that is not true. I know that I am the best friend she'll ever have; maybe Rhett secondly, because he is kind to her when Pa isn't looking, putting a sweater around her shoulders, helping her build a fire, giving her the change from his pockets.

"Time to close." The waitress strokes my hair. "You liked that pie, sweetie?"

"Yes, thank you."

I would like to go with the waitress Gladys. I would like to lean into her hands and close my eyes, be led through the rainy streets to where I imagine she must live in a walk-up apartment. She'll have a big radio and listen to *Lum and Abner* and *Amos and Andy*, and she'll laugh, even if she's alone. She'll have boxes of sugar almonds and a single lamp that gives off just enough light.

I would like to know what is going to happen tomorrow and the next day.

When Hari and Kari were three, the farmer's wife asked him to kill them. "Sever them in two the way God intended," the farmer's wife instructed. "Bury them under separate trees."

But the farmer didn't obey.

Instead, he got on a train and took them to Cleveland, where a traveling carnival was stopping for a big show. The head carny asked how much they ate and gave the farmer two dollars for them.

The farmer wept as he rode the train home and watched the rippling fields of wheat from the window. "It was God's will," his wife repeated, as he stumbled in the door.

If you ask me, it's bad luck to try to second-guess God's will. When Pa does it, it never goes well.

Every time Hari and Kari told their stories, the bearded lady cried. She wasn't really a lady, but a man so fat he looked like a lady. His story was also sad. His whole life he believed he should be a girl. His whole life his pa beat him for it, until finally he ran away and joined the show.

What time must it be? We're the only ones left. The cook is scrubbing down the grill. When I'm up on my tightrope, there is no such thing as time. There is only air, the lightness of it.

Tonight I wore my pink costume with my lace parasol, and danced on the rope like a ballerina. When Pa told the people that hell is an endless pit, I teetered and pretended to fall. They gasped as I righted myself and back-flipped in the air. "Come to me as little children," Pa shouted.

Gladys collects the plates. She does it like she means it. She sets a scrap of paper on the table; Ma checks it to make sure she didn't charge us for the pie. Pa pulls out the collection box. Because I don't feel like leaving the warm diner and heading out into the rain, because we're sleeping in some old lady's barn, because I feel mad for reasons I don't even know, I say, "I thought you collected that money for the poor."

"Well, ain't we the poor?" Pa pulls another cigarette from his pocket.

Hari and Kari grew to enjoy their life in the traveling carnival. They had each other, of course, and they became friends with the other performers, but they never forgot the farmer or stopped worrying about him having to live with a woman who had such a hard heart.

These are just two people (or one) whom I've met on my many travels, and who've disappeared on me like it was them, and not us, who were such fly-by-nights.

2

LISTEN TO YOUR FATHER WHO BEGOT YOU.

—*PROVERBS*

We leave the next morning in our broken-down car. Pa says we need to find a town where there's a factory and workers. After a day of labor, a paycheck in their pockets, their stomachs full, they will look for another need met. God as savior. God as entertainment. "This will be our best revival yet," Pa says.

It's a funny word, revival. It reminds me of a drowned lady having air blown into her mouth. We never go to the same place twice. What is there to revive?

The streets are dark with rain, but the sky itself is clear. We live our life by weather. We have been snowed in, rained out, and dusted over one time when the dust storm was so heavy we couldn't make our way in the car. Today, the fear is that if the rain starts up again, the road will turn to mud.

Rhett stands on the running board. He watches for signs that might direct our travels. From the look on his face, you'd think that he was skiing at a fancy resort instead of being blown around by an icy wind.

Once we've navigated our course, Rhett climbs back in the car and plops down next to me. He smiles and does tricks with string before falling into a deep sleep. Sometimes he mumbles from within his dreams; it is the only way I know that he has a voice.

I look out the back window at the few shops that aren't boarded shut and the diner where we had dinner, and wave good-bye. It's a habit I have. I pretend that there is someone waving back: a lady standing on a porch in a printed dress and apron, an aunt or grandma, a man in a hat and vest smoking a pipe, a grandpa, a bearded lady.

"Look, there's the school." Ma points as we pass a small white building with a flag. "It looks like a nice one. So many of them have been shut down. I wish . . ."

That's all she needs to say; Pa knows where she's headed, for she often talks about her enjoyment of school, her belief that I should go too.

"What's she gonna learn? That man is descended from apes?" Pa pounds the dashboard and he is off on one of his favorite subjects; the scientist's attempts to murder God.

I have seen an illustration that shows an ape all slumped over, then slowly standing straighter, looking more and more like a person until he is wearing a suit and hat. Whether we came from apes, or clay—the hard soil of the earth—it doesn't seem much different to me; *both* are miraculous, like there is something else driving life, and that something is invisible.

"That wasn't a bad town." Ma's voice is high, tense. "A person could live in a town like that, get to know people, settle down."

"That town makes Sodom and Gomorrah look like an advertisement for Paradise. It was a sin-pit."

It's hard for me to make a connection, though, between the barbershop and diner and the sinfulness he is going on about. It gets harder and harder to make sense of what he says, and I wonder if Ma feels the same. She told me that when she first met Pa, his voice was sweet as caramel. It sure is sour now.

I put my hands over my ears and lean up against the window. A thin crack runs right down the middle, but somehow it holds together. Ma once told me that there are miracles everywhere; they're just very hard to see. Here is a visible one.

Ma has said that without the car we would be "goners." The car has housed us many times when the weather was bad and we didn't have enough money for a room. And it brings us to places where we are new for a day or two (America loves novelty, Pa says), but the car is getting as tired as Ma. When Pa changes gears there is a grinding sound. The door is rusted and part of the front end has dropped off.

Within a few moments the shops shrink to doll-house size, then disappear into nothing. The past has just passed again.

In better days, back in the twenties, Pa had bigger crowds; sometimes there were rich people. And he wore a velvet suit. Once, when I was three, an old lady who needed a hand with her soul let us stay in her fancy house for two whole months. She gave Ma a silk dress and put bows in my hair. This was when Ma still sang and *she* was the attraction, not me.

The rich lady gave Pa the car. She had bought it for her son, to keep him from running off, but he left any-way. She was afraid of the car. She asked Pa, "Do you think it's the devil's work, to come up with something that can move people so fast and far?"

"Let me take it off your hands," Pa said. "I know how to dispose of it."

The rich lady offered to keep me when they left. She said that without her son the house was too quiet and that my gold curls made her think of an angel. Ma considered it. She liked the idea of me living in one place, to grow in any direction that I pleased and not be stopped by the confines of a car or tent, but Pa said no, that Ma's voice was going sour and they would need something else. That something else just might be me, he said.

He had never paid much mind to me until the week before, when a man had come to him and said, "Your daughter is a beauty. Enough to make a believer out of anyone."

"Yeah," Pa had agreed, "I should work her in somehow."

I still remember the first time. I wasn't yet four. Pa tied a rope across two poles. "The air will hold you up. It is made of angel's breath. Just let your feet touch and the rest of you will float."

He was my pa. He wore a blue velvet suit. I believed him, and I did it.

"She's a child," Ma argued, but was silenced by Pa's glare.

At first Pa held my hand. Then, when the tightrope became higher, he used a pole to help me balance. Soon he just walked beside me while I learned to twirl and spin, to drop and rise on the rope as if I had been born on it.

I practiced from the time I woke up until lunchtime. Ma often said that I could walk the tightrope in my sleep. She thought Pa was being mean to me, but I liked the tightrope, then. The things Pa said that made no sense on the ground made more sense in the sky. I could see how angels might hover above the earth, like balloons filled with helium, how they might see everything going on and wish it was better, but not be able to touch the ground.

I could imagine myself any way I wanted up there: getting in my own airplane and flying around like Amelia Earhart, opening my own candy shop, or following the other girls in their blue coats and hats, their satchels, their lunch pails, and entering a schoolhouse where the teacher would slice facts and make them bleed meaning.

I could picture myself like everyone else.

How long ago was this? I've kind of lost track. I guess the passage of time by the weather and the changes in my body, the way flat places are growing rounder even as I sit in the car, and I wonder: How will these changes affect my balance?

"Moses himself couldn't convince me!" Pa erupts. All I know is that if Moses couldn't convince him, then Ma definitely can't.

Moses is one of Pa's heroes because he could walk up to a sea and it would split right open for him.

God came to Moses in a burning bush and told him, "You will lead my people out of slavery," but Moses wondered how he could do that. Who would believe that Moses saw the vision of God? "Besides," Moses told God, "I stutter."

"Take your brother Aaron," God instructed. "He speaks really well."

Moses argued over and over with God. Finally, Moses said, "Please send someone else!"

Pa says Moses didn't want to lead the people out of Egypt because he was too humble to believe that he could do it, but I think maybe he just wasn't happy about spending all those years hiking around in the desert with a bunch of whiners. Or maybe he knew that God would offer him the Promised Land, and then make him die before he set one foot in it.

ॐ

While Pa is as skinny as Ma, Rhett is beefy. I lean against his big, warm shoulder. "Stay with us, Rhett," I whisper. "I hate it when you leave. It's no fun."

His arm flops over me, but he doesn't wake up.

There have been other folks who have traveled with us. There was once a lady from New Mexico. We met her in Oklahoma. She had a rattlesnake that she kept in a cage. She'd take it out and it would slide around her body, as meek as a kitten. This showed God's favoritism toward her, she said. At anyone else, the snake would strike.

The snake was responsible for the death of two of her three husbands. The third one had just been no good. He had stolen all her turquoise jewelry one night and crept away along the riverbed by the light of the moon. She never heard from him again, although she got a postcard from a friend saying he'd gone to California to build movie sets.

Snake Lady could speak in tongues. Her eyes would roll back in her head and ancient languages would crawl like snakes from her mouth. And she could heal. Pa has never had the healing touch. When he tries, half the time he knocks people over, whacking them on the forehead with the palm of his hand, shouting "Heal" with a Southern accent, even though he's from Chicago. Nothing makes a crowd madder than being promised they'll be cured, then having some preacher knock 'em over and sprain their ankle or their wrist.

But Snake Lady had a softer touch. A boy might come limping up and she'd massage his leg and whisper to him like he was her boyfriend and he'd go skipping away.

Pa said she *asked* to be dropped off in New Orleans, but Ma said he made her leave because she had the spirit and Pa was jealous of her talents.

Ma admitted to me once that Pa used to have the spirit. At night, he would lie awake, his eyes shining, and recite scripture. It was like he was in a trance, Ma said. In the morning, he didn't remember a thing. And it used to be he'd share what little he had with anyone like he was Jesus or St. Francis. But somewhere on the path between hunger and disappointment the spirit just took a different road and never visited him again. It was then that Pa turned mean.

After Snake Lady, a cousin of Ma's ran away from home and joined us. He was fifteen. His name was Big Ben. The joke of it was that he was about as little as you could get. Fifteen and he was all of four feet high and about sixty pounds. He didn't like being called Big

Ben. He said Big Ben was a clock in London, England, and he was no good at telling time. But it was his name and he was stuck with it.

In his sleep, Rhett mumbles. When Aimee Semple McPherson was only nineteen she walked into a church, opened her mouth, and spoke in tongues. She was that filled with the spirit.

Since then she has healed more than five thousand blind, deaf, paralyzed, and heartbroken people. Of these, it must be the heartbroken that are worst off.

From beneath the gray blanket of air, atop the rumbling road, I fall into sleep. Usually, I dream that a voice comes to guide me. When I ask the voice who it is, it answers: a rock, a spiderweb, a branch, a white bead on an abacus. It has never once said God.

But today I dream of falling. I am on the rope when I grow very, very heavy and I fall into the crowd of God-struck people. The pale leaves of their faces tilt up and their white limbs rise to catch me as I am passed among the river of their hands, one to another, am kept by them, am kept.

3

I SHALL NOT WANT.

—*PSALM 23*

When I wake up, we are in Detroit, the city where cars are made and factories, like steel dragons, breathe fire from their mouths. In the downtown, buildings crowd together. A horn blows and we watch workers pour out of a factory onto the street.

"Have those men been working all night?" Ma asks.

"They're treated like ants," Pa says. "We'll set up in that empty lot."

"How do you know it's not private property?"

"I don't see a sign. Do you see a sign?"

"Remember what happened in Raleigh," Ma says.

"What happened?" I ask.

"Never you mind."

Each town feels different. It's as if they are people and some of them are kindly and sweet, some stingy, and some downright mean. This one is none too cheerful. The men coming out of the factory look like they think that every day of their lives will have gray, freezing weather like this. Ants, at least, can huddle together in the ground.

Even Pa can sense it. "This is about as promising as a poorhouse after a tornado."

"Haven't we been here before?" Ma twists a strand of her hair.

Someday we may run out of towns.

"It's Cleveland you're thinking of," Pa says. "Isn't it?"

"I have a bad feeling. . . ."

A group of people is playing instruments in front of a barbershop. "Salvation Army," Pa sneers. He pulls over to the curb.

I jump out of the car and run ahead to see the Salvation Army. I love the way the ladies and men are dressed alike, like soldiers, so it's hard to tell one from the other. They play their instruments as if they don't care what anybody in the world thinks of them, which is a good thing, because they play very badly. I join the small crowd watching them.

Within five minutes, trouble arises. A man heaves a rotten tomato at the lady playing a little drum. "Heathen!" the man shouts. The lady stops long enough to wipe the tomato off her face, then she drums even louder than before.

A boy, not much bigger than me, throws what looks like wet bread. Then the whole crowd is yelling at the Salvation Army people, calling them names that even I've never heard.

One man grabs Drum Lady and shakes her up and down like she's a piggy bank. Another tosses an egg at the trumpet player. It misses him and hits a man standing behind. He chases the man who threw it. Soon there is yelling and scuffling all round. A cop on the corner just stands and watches the whole thing.

Rhett tugs on my arm and pulls me away from the crowd.

"Get over here, June." Pa yanks me away from Rhett. Rhett's face gets real red, like it does when he's mad. He just stays right where he is; he doesn't come along with us. "We don't want to get mixed up with the likes of them," Pa says.

"I think we better try someplace else," Ma suggests.

"We need to pick up some cash first."

"Why were those people being so mean?" I ask.

"The Salvation Army will convert anyone," Pa explains. "Drunks, prostitutes, people who ain't fit for the world. The church folks don't like them."

"Church folks don't like us either," Ma whispers, but so quiet that only I hear it.

"Mary Magdalene was a prostitute," I explore.

"Yes," Pa agrees.

"Jesus liked her."

"Uh-huh."

"Why are people so hard on prostitutes? It doesn't seem that those ladies have much choice," I offer. "If they don't marry someone, or are rich, how do they make a living?"

"Shut your mouth!" Ma slaps my face. "Imagine, you saying such a thing."

When Ma slaps my face, I always feel like she's slapping her own; don't ask me why. Still, it stings, and reminds me that I can't say what comes to mind, especially not when Ma and Pa are together.

"You'll make her face red for the show!" Pa admonishes her.

"I'm so hungry I'm shaking," Ma says by way of apology.

"We'll tie up the rope in that square over there, June. You can practice and it'll give folks a little preview."

My neck is sore from being squished into the car. My feet are cold. My empty stomach makes me wish I hadn't had such a casual attitude toward my supper last night.

"Let's at least get a cup of coffee, Alfred," Ma begs, "or some soup. I didn't sleep a wink last night. As loud as that cow was mooing, I thought it was going to step right on top of me."

"We should'a milked it," Pa says.

"I'm hungry too," I complain.

"No practice. No food." I can tell the treatment of the Salvation Army people has made him uneasy. "Agnes, did you see the way she wobbled last night just at the moment she was supposed to be still?"

I freeze inside, although somehow my legs keep walking. This is the first time I've received anything but praise from Pa about my performance. But I must admit, I felt it too. Just when I should've been perfectly still, my foot slipped a bit to the side.

"Besides, we got to get our advertising up."

"Where's Rhett?" Ma starts.

"Who the hell knows?" Pa hates it when she fusses over Rhett. "Maybe he's run off again."

"Oh, no. It's been a while since he's done that. He wouldn't . . ."

"We'll do without him."

I don't say anything about where Rhett is. If they were nicer to him, then maybe he wouldn't get mad and take off. I just hope he doesn't go too far.

We walk around the damp gray town, pasting leaflets to windows. Pa writes in the location of our tent with a pencil.

He agrees to stop for breakfast, finally, but says I will do without lunch on account of my refusal to practice.

"Let's stop at that Woolworth's," Ma says. "I need to buy us some soap, too."

There's just about anything you might want in the Woolworth's. There are ironing boards and irons, rubber boots, cleaning supplies, long johns, flannel pajamas, slippers, babies' socks and bottles—a wonderful array of things I would like to look at, let alone buy, but Pa drags us impatiently toward the counter. "You can have an egg sandwich," he tells me. "It's fifteen cents."

"I want a cup of coffee," I say, "with sugar and cream."

"No coffee. It'll stain your teeth."

"Let her drink something hot," Ma says, still trying to make up for the slap. "The cold gets right through to your bones, and her new costume is scant for this kind of weather."

"That's the beauty of it," Pa says, ordering a sandwich and milk for me and coffee and doughnuts for him and Ma. He never asks Ma what she wants.

The food feels so good in me. I eat every bite, taking advantage of my swivel stool to feast my eyes on the colored fabrics and threads.

Within a few moments, four of the Salvation Army people that we saw earlier come in. There are two men and two women. One of the men has a black eye. Drum Lady has been washed off pretty well; just a few tomato seeds cling to the shoulder of her uniform. She puts their collection box on the counter.

For people who were just beat up, they seem in a pretty good mood.

"They say the autoworkers will march next month," says one of the men.

"That's so?" Black-Eyed Man says.

"A march in March," Drum Lady adds by way of a joke.

"President Hoover himself couldn't stop this one. The men are organizing."

"After seeing what they can do with vegetables," says Drum Lady, "I wouldn't want to be there when they cast the first stone."

They all laugh like that's the funniest thing ever said.

Black-Eyed Man says, "Hoover's too busy going after the likes of Al Capone to bother with hungry workers."

"Still, I'd rather not get on Capone's bad side."

Capone is the most famous gangster in the world. Pa says that on a scale of 1 to 10 for sinners Capone is 100. He has these parties where he feeds the guests dinner, then for dessert has their heads smashed in with baseball bats. But what if the president of the United States could be doing more to help folks than he is? Doesn't that make him a sinner too?

"Let's go." Pa stands.

"Please, Alfred," Ma begs, "let's have another cup of coffee."

"I don't share a counter with the likes of them." He nods toward the Salvation Army.

"They're Christians too," Ma says, offering a rare argument. "And they do a lot of good."

It must be nice to have musical instruments to play so that people can hear you all over town, even if they do throw stuff at you. And it must be nice to belong together as a group and wear matching clothes.

"June!" Pa nudges me off of the stool. "Sleep your way through life and what'll you end up with?"

"Dreams?" I suggest, but he just rolls his eyes. He doesn't like my answer one bit.

THE SACRED STONES LIE SCATTERED
AT THE HEAD OF EVERY STREET.

—*LAMENTATIONS*

I've been wondering what happened to Big Ben. He was with us for almost a year before he got lonely for his ma and sister. It was one of those times when Rhett was gone and we didn't know where he went. Pa thought Big Ben could help set up the tent and hang leaflets, but Big Ben tended to get things wrong. Like he would hang the leaflets backward so that the blank side showed. Or set up the tent cockeyed. When he tried to help Ma cook breakfast one morning, he set fire to the eggs.

"That boy's got marbles in his head," Pa said.

Big Ben wanted to work on automobiles—that

was his dream—and he imagined having his own shop and living above it with a wife and three or four children. At first, he fancied himself a preacher like Pa, but he couldn't remember his scripture. He got confused and thought it was Abraham who took the creatures on the ark and Noah whose bright idea it was to eat from the Tree of Knowledge. He could never remember if it was Judas or Peter who betrayed Jesus, planting a kiss on him in one of the most mixed gestures of affection ever.

Just before he went back to his ma, Big Ben told me that he was too scared to be a preacher. "I think the Holy Spirit is in the lungs," he had said. "When you use all that breath talking about God, it plum escapes."

It was the smartest thing Big Ben ever said. I'd noticed it myself—how the more Pa preached, the emptier he seemed. It made me wonder if the words tumbling out of Pa's mouth was all the holiness he had and he was squandering it.

From where I hide behind the tent, I peek out at the crowd. It is bigger than in the last town, where I'm sure the pouring rain washed away even the wish to be saved. The crowd is mostly women, which is typical, but a couple of factory men are out there too, still in their work clothes and looking about as happy as pigs on the way to slaughter.

If someone hits me with a tomato, I hope I can keep my balance. One reason why I'm here is to keep people not only interested, but behaving.

I climb the ladder. Rhett has returned; he shines the light up on my rope. The spectators gaze toward me, toward heaven. We always start with an empty rope and let them wait a good minute. Then slowly, like an invalid woman, I pull myself up the ladder. Like I said, places are starting to round out on me. I can feel my skin straining beneath my skimpy costume. My hair is tied up on my head and my lips rouged, and I never ever look down.

As I take a deep breath, my ribs expand to the point of bursting. It's like my ribs are a birdcage; my heart, the bird.

Although it is freezing, I wear my green paper hula skirt and my gold sweater trimmed with colored flowers. When I do a cartwheel on the rope, the paper grass gets into my eyes. Some men move right under me as if they want to look inside of my body at my innards.

When I spin and pretend to fall, the crowd lets out

a cry, like babies gasping for their first breath. A woman shrieks, "Amen!" And only then do I know the show is going to go just fine, because a group of people respond as one, and no one has ever gotten mad after an "Amen."

This is the opening. All eyes on me. But then Rhett swings the light onto Pa and I crouch down and wait in the shadows. Pa preaches from Matthew 7:13, about how narrow the gate is for those who will find salvation. Meanwhile, the gate to sin is as wide and vast as the sea. The easiest thing in the world is to dive in for a swim.

Matthew is handy when Pa is speaking to the poor, to those who find it difficult to part with their few coins. There are plenty of passages about not keeping treasures and about not worrying about the care of the body.

To empty your pockets is an act of faith.

Then Pa tells the parable from Luke. When the rich fool hoards his treasures, God comes right along and smacks him dead.

When Pa reminds the crowd of Christ's torment, his slow crucifixion, Amen Lady begins to weep.

It makes me pretty sad too, no matter how many times I hear the story, although I must admit that when I think about God giving up His favorite Son to be heckled, tortured, and nailed to a cross, it makes my parents' behavior seem a lot more explicable.

Ma passes the salvation box around. "Every penny of this," Pa trumpets, "will go to the poor, to those who don't have jobs to go to, homes to live in, or food to eat. And now my child, June, blessed with the Holy Spirit, will walk on air."

Pa begins a hymn. His voice sounds like an old door creaking at its hinges. Amen Lady sings with all her heart in a voice that reminds me of an opera singer meeting her death in some strange way: being pulled apart by the rack, or thrown into a volcano by natives who believe it will assuage its wrath.

There are about thirty people tonight. It's one of our biggest crowds ever. I hover above them and dance as best I can to the mixed rhythms of their song.

5

EVERY SEVEN YEARS, GOD FORGETS YOUR NAME.

— *Old saying*

Finally, the show over, I get to climb down. Most people leave, but a few hang around to talk to Pa. Ma ducks behind the tent to count the collections; she gives them to Rhett for safekeeping. Rhett fetches another sweater for Ma from the car, then he walks away into the field to smoke; he doesn't like crowds.

"That preacher your dad?" a boy asks me. He's got straight brown hair that hangs in his eyes like the fringe of a curtain and big fat freckles on his face. He looks to be about my age, but he's a good bit taller.

"Uh-huh," I say.

"That's my mother who's talking to him," he explains, pointing to Amen Lady. "She's gotten religion since my dad died. She thinks God will bring him back somehow."

"She sings real loud," I offer by way of a compliment.

"What's that thing you're wearing?"

"It's a hula skirt. It's Hawaiian."

"Can I touch it?"

"Okay."

"That's paper," he says, disappointed. "I thought it was grass."

"My ma made it. If this were Hawaii it would be real grass and my top would be coconut shells."

"Really?"

"Yeah, and maybe I'd have a hat made out of pineapple or something."

Kids usually ask me about how I float on air, but he just fixes his gray eyes on me. "You're different. So am I. My dad used to tell me I take things too seriously. Plus, you got the prettiest hair I ever seen. It's like someone put sunlight in it."

"It's just blond. Haven't you ever seen blond hair?"

"I got licorice." He holds out a black rope. "You want some?"

"Okay."

We walk over to where our car is and sit on the running board.

"How'd your pa die?" I ask.

"The mine where he was working caved in. He was in charge of the whole thing. He thought it was a good job, but it killed him."

"That's too bad."

"Yeah. I miss him, even though he used to give me a hiding every other day."

"Are my teeth black?" Nothing peeves Pa more than having me look messy with folks around.

"Yeah."

"I better not have any more."

"Do you travel around all over?"

"Yeah."

"We're gonna travel. Now that my dad's gone, we're gonna move to my mom's sister's house in Seattle. I'm glad."

"I get sick of traveling. Every place starts to seem the same."

"Hawaii wouldn't seem the same," he argues, trailing his finger along the running board. "China wouldn't. We had friends who went there as missionaries and both of them died within a month."

"Aimee Semple McPherson went there with her husband and he died too."

"Who's that?"

"A lady preacher." Some people sure don't know much. "She's so famous, she's like a movie star. One time she was even kidnapped. She went swimming in the ocean and someone made off with her."

"I'm not much interested in movie stars. I don't think talkies will last. Do you? The radio's so much better, 'cause you get to imagine how everyone looks."

I shrug. The boy's thin, freckled face, his sweater and pleated trousers make me feel somehow sad. Even if I like him, I'll never see him again.

"I got a hole in my leg," he says, as if it's something he's just noticed. "Wanna see it?"

"Okay."

"You gotta give me a nickel."

"Why?"

"So I'll show you."

"How'd you get the hole?"

"A bullet. It went clear through my leg."

"Who shot you?"

"Huh?"

"I said, who shot you? If you got a bullet, someone must've shot you."

He wipes his mouth. Black juice spreads on his hand, which he then wipes on his trousers. "My dad. It was an accident. He meant to shoot the dog 'cause it killed our chickens. But I loved the dog, so I went to save him, and he shot me in the leg by accident."

I picture a tunnel going through his leg. It would be dark and empty; a train could come through anytime. "I don't have a nickel," I say.

"Then you can't see."

"You got to see *me* up there, walking the tightrope. I didn't charge *you!*"

He thinks about that for a moment.

"What happened to the dog?" I ask.

"My dad still shot him. He shot me, then he told me to move and he shot the dog. Then he had to ride on a horse to get the doctor, 'cause we didn't have our jalopy yet." He pulls up his pant leg and there on his shin is a little puny round scar.

"That's not a hole!"

"Well, it used to be."

"That's just a little circle!"

He rolls down his pant leg. "It's gotten smaller over time. You should've seen it at first. My next-door neighbor took one look at it and got sick all over the place."

I see Pa trying to pull himself away from the boy's ma.

"What's your name?" he asks.

"June."

"That's a month."

"That's when I was born."

"Oh."

"What's your name?"

"Theodore."

"That's a nice name. It sounds kind of important."

"That's the name of the next president, my mom says."

"Really?"

"I guess you must believe in God and all, having your dad be a preacher."

"Sometimes I believe in God."

"Like when?"

"Like when I'm by a stream or in the woods. Or when I see something real pretty like a cardinal."

"Maybe you'll be a preacher like that lady."

"Aimee McPherson? No way," I say, although I know that is Pa's plan for me. *I'm grooming her to take over the family business,* I've heard him say.

"I don't believe in God," Theodore whispers.

"Why not?"

"Look around you. Everyone poor and suffering. What kind of God is that?"

"You don't look poor."

"We're not."

"Maybe God just lets folks do things their own way, and that doesn't work out too well."

"Yeah, I guess no one wants to be bossed around."

"There you are!" Ma yells at me.

Theodore touches my hair. "I'm gonna marry you, June," he says. "Someday!"

The way he says it, I almost believe him.

He turns once more before his ma takes his arm and leads him toward their car. It's a nice car. It looks brand new. I bet he's got a nice house.

"Get something warm on, June," Ma scolds.

Theodore's car drives away. Rhett's cigarette tip glows like a firefly in the distance.

"How much, Agnes?" Pa asks.

"Six dollars."

It's the most we've gotten in a long time.

"That woman gave me twenty." Pa grins.

That makes Ma light right up. "You reached her tonight, Alfred." She takes the twenty from his hand.

ᕍ

As if to acknowledge the end of our show, the moon ducks behind a big black cloud.

I think we are alone, but all of a sudden, a man steps out from behind our car. He is very tall with a long face and no chin. He is wearing a gray suit and white gloves. He reminds me of a man I once saw working in a bank. When the man gave us our money his hands were white as snow.

Behind the well-dressed man are two others. They wear blue uniforms with gold buttons and matching blue hats, and have long sticks tucked into their belts.

Quickly, Ma puts the twenty in the front of her dress.

"You are under arrest," one of the policemen says. As the other reaches for Pa, the moon reappears, shining like a searchlight.

6

THEN THE LORD GOD FORMED MAN
FROM THE DUST OF THE GROUND.

—*GENESIS*

Do you ever look up at the stars at night? They seem to grow like zinnias in the sky. When a shooting star explodes, you are supposed to wish, but I'm always too busy watching those falling petals.

Hari and Kari once told me that the bearded lady could move objects with his eyes. A candlestick or a piece of lace would rise in the air. His will was so great, his concentration so fierce, that his gaze became a force of energy.

I have seen objects move when I am lying in the car, unable to sleep. I've seen a stack of twigs float straight into the air on a windless night and a tambourine shake across the passenger seat all by itself.

Tonight, I gaze up at the sky and find a star. I wait for it to fall so I can wish, but it doesn't budge an inch. It just blooms there.

It could be that the rumble of the earth shook the tambourine and that what I thought were twigs were actually night birds taking flight. It could be that God, exhausted from His worries, from man's griping and bad ways, has rested His eyes, and fallen asleep.

Pa's been in trouble before. Once, a man came at him with a poker because he believed Pa had looked at his wife funny. Another time, a woman said Pa stole her money and some folks chased our car down the road. Another time, a lady told Pa that folks were planning to lynch him. They said he'd collected money for a hospital fund but he never gave the hospital the money. Then there was the time a group of Ku Klux Klan thought we were hiding a black man; I don't know why. They pitched kerosene on our tent and lit it on fire. That was the last time Pa preached in the South.

He has been questioned by police, beaten up by other preachers, shoved down the stairs by a priest, chased through a field by a herd of goats, capsized in a fishing boat as he rowed from bank to bank to spread the Word. He's slept overnight in jail twice. "Look what they did to Jesus," he told Ma one time as she nursed his wounds. "Can I expect less?"

Ma said Pa is just being punished for being good, but it seems to me that he makes a lot of promises about the money we take in, like that it will be given to the poor, the crippled, or the downtrodden. Then he just keeps it for himself.

Pa has always told our audience about the meekness and mildness of Jesus, but to me he says that Jesus was a rabble-rouser. He argued with important politicians, entered a temple and turned over the tables of the moneylenders. Jesus yelled a good bit. And Pa said he doesn't blame Him at all, since people are so stupid and irritating. It was like Jesus was a singer and everyone had their hands over their ears.

After the two other men take Pa away, the tall man tells Ma we have to clear off the property. She should come to the courthouse tomorrow, where Pa will see the judge.

Rhett opens the car door and motions for me to climb in. Then he gets into the driver's seat.

"I thought this was the place where we had trouble before. I told him we might have been here." Ma settles into the passenger seat. "Who could forget Detroit? It's the ugliest place on earth." Ma never speaks to Rhett when Pa's around. "How ever will I be able to sleep knowing Alfred is in jail?"

Rhett shrugs.

"Just once, it would be nice to know what you think!"

He looks back at her. It's almost like he's saying, *You know exactly what I think.*

"You could at least give a person some company, throw a few words out there to fill the air. Ever think of that? Difficult. That's what you are. Find someplace that's not private property, so we can park and sleep in peace."

"Can't we get something to eat first? I didn't have any lunch," I ask.

"I couldn't eat a bite knowing your pa's in trouble," Ma scolds, "and I don't know how you could! Besides, we want to be fresh and looking our best when we go to the court tomorrow. The judge will be more kindly when he sees what decent people we are."

We clear off the land and drive to the outskirts of town. Rhett sets up part of the tent against the car for him. He bundles me up in the backseat. Ma sleeps in front.

"Now I lay me down to sleep," Ma starts the bed-time prayer, "I pray the Lord, my soul to keep. If I should die before I wake, I pray the Lord my soul to take."

I have to admit I've never liked this prayer. Who wants to think about dying in their sleep, even if dying is supposed to be the end-all be-all?

Ma closes her eyes. I roll down the window to call out good night to Rhett, but he is already snoring, his mumbling voice spilling out the same word over and over. And the word is *Mine*.

7

DID I NOT WEEP FOR THOSE WHOSE DAY WAS HARD?
WAS NOT MY SOUL GRIEVED FOR THE POOR?

—*JOB*

There's a lot of jealousy in the Bible, especially among brothers. Like Cain, who murders his brother, Abel, then has to wander around with a mark on his head. Or Jacob, who is jealous of his father's favoritism toward his brother, Esau, and pretends to be Esau so he can get his father's deathbed blessing. Then there's Jacob's son, Joseph. His brothers are so jealous of him that they sell him into slavery.

It was Joseph I dreamed about last night, or at least his coat. I was walking down a path lined with trees when a beautiful coat appeared out of thin air. As I got nearer to the coat, it began to speak. "I will tell you the secret you seek," the coat said, and I knew that I would receive the answer of God. At that exact moment, Ma gave me a shove, and told me to wake up.

As Rhett drives us toward the courthouse, I see a soup kitchen with a line stretched halfway down the block. How I would love to be standing in that line, pushed between the bodies of the hungry people. It feels only right that poor folks should have each other for company as they eat cooked oats and drink coffee and listen to some preacher tell them about their sin and folly. The people you meet and the stories you hear in the soup kitchens are almost as good as those from the carnival.

Last time we went to one, there was a man who had been so rich he had gold and diamond faucets in his bathrooms. On their anniversary, he and his wife took a bath in expensive champagne. He made his wealth by inventing a valve used to distill liquor, then he invested everything in the stock market. This is the American way, he told us. No kings or queens, just honest hard work and "an enterprising spirit." But prohibition has ruined the country, he said. Without drink, Americans have become mean in spirit. And those who still drink are at the mercy of the thugs, the bootleggers, and the gangsters, like Al Capone.

On the day the stock market crashed, he phoned his wife: "We are starting over from scratch. Broke. We still have love," he told her sadly. On the phone, she agreed.

When he got home, though, his wife had disappeared. Her furs, the silver, the china, anything of value that could be carried away, was gone. She even took the bathroom faucets.

Suddenly, the man felt ashamed of his wasteful habits. He saw that his wife had loved not him, but his money. And what kind of love is that?

He thought about going to the top of his house, where the roof had recently been adorned with copper. "I was going to dive off the roof," he told me. Instead, he walked out the door and down to the train station. He climbed onto a freight car with a bunch of other men. Most of them stared at him because of his fancy clothes, but one man gave him a hand up. He took that hand as a sign, and he's been riding the rails ever since.

I don't remember his name, but I liked him. He had a mustache that grew all the way down to his shoulders.

Ma didn't like him, though. She said when a man wears a mustache, it's because he has something to hide.

"But Rhett has a mustache," I had said.

"Exactly."

Rhett parks the car downtown. Ma instructs him to find a new tent location and hang the leaflets for the show tonight. She seems pretty sure Pa will be freed.

When Ma turns to walk away, Rhett stops her and points to me, then makes a gesture of eating and drinking.

"She's comin' with me," Ma says. "It'll get more sympathy from the judge. We'll have breakfast later. It's just trespassing, that's all. There'll be a fine. Good thing that woman gave us twenty dollars. The Lord works mysteriously."

The idea of a fine makes my stomach hurt. What if it takes every cent? There'll be nothing left to buy breakfast.

Rhett motions for her to stay. He disappears around the corner and comes back with an apple, which he gives me.

"You're impossible," Ma complains at him, but she doesn't sound like she's really mad.

The court is in a fancy building, with big columns in front of it. So much of Detroit's buildings are blackened with soot, but this one is clean and white. Despite being full of people, the courtroom is cold. The wooden seats remind me of church pews. I scan the walls, half expecting to see a crucified Jesus. Instead, there is a sign, which says LET NO MAN TAKE JUSTICE INTO HIS HANDS. It makes me think again of Joseph in the Bible, how his father, Jacob, gave him a coat of many colors and how his brothers sold him into slavery and pretended to his father that he was dead. Is that taking justice into your hands?

Another saying of Snake Lady's was "With friends like that, who needs enemies?" Well, with brothers like that, who needs family?

Pa is led out and made to swear on a Bible. He looks so small in the big courtroom. He takes a seat, his hands in his lap, his head lowered, as if there are words on his hands and he's trying to read them.

I don't really follow the proceedings of the courtroom because there is too much to distract me. There's a woman with a hat covered in peacock feathers, a baby who looks like a pig, and a man with a black cat on his shoulder. I had a cat once when I was little; he was the best listener in the world. He was orange with white paws. I called him Marble. He slept on my neck. He liked to play with Ma's ball of yarn. We had him two years, then one night, when times were getting harder, Pa sold him to a lady who came to one of the shows. She took a fancy to Marble, who was sitting so nicely in Ma's lap, and she offered Pa fifty cents. He didn't think twice about selling him.

The word *trespassing* is mentioned. Pa pleads ignorance. He calls the judge "sir" and keeps his most respectful tone. Just when I see Ma sigh in relief, the judge says, "Now there is the matter of the warrant. . . ."

"We *have* been here before," Ma gasps, and squeezes my hand so hard it hurts.

I'm not sure what a warrant is, but from the look on Pa's face, it isn't good. I hear dates, places, and some words I don't quite understand. Pa seems to shrink within his own skin.

In the Bible, Joseph is imprisoned on false charges. A woman pretends that he has made advances. Eventually, he finds his way out of his troubles by his ability to interpret dreams. And despite all that his brothers did to him, Joseph forgives them. *Turn the other cheek,* as Jesus said. *Judge ye not, lest ye be judged.*

I remind myself to pay attention, but then the lady takes off the peacock hat and sets it on the seat. The cat stares at the long feathers, then leaps over the seat and jumps on the hat. The woman squeals. People say cats have nine lives, but I wonder how they know that, being as we only have one, and most of us waste it anyway.

By the time the commotion is over and I look back at Pa, he is being led away by a policeman. As if in response, Pig Baby starts howling even louder. Pa's back is bent forward as he disappears behind the door.

"Five months!" Ma screams, and faints onto the floor. The policeman and another man try to lift her to her feet.

"Come with me, girl." It is the tall man from last night. "We'll see to your mother. She needs a doctor."

"I'm going with her."

"I'm your friend." He leans toward me, offers me a mint from his pocket, and slides it into my mouth with a skill that makes me wonder.

8

THOU SHALT NOT COVET THY NEIGHBOR'S GOODS.

—The tenth commandment

You would think that Hari and Kari would live happily ever after, once they found their place in the traveling circus. But life isn't so simple. Their health was often bad, their organs strained by the weight of two heads, two sets of thoughts. They had stomachaches and bad circulation. Their feet were swollen.

Hari fell in love with the incredible shrinking woman. Her name was Lila Lou. She weighed eighty-five pounds. Dehydrated, she could collapse in on herself and fold up into almost nothing. But Kari didn't like her at all. He wore earplugs and hummed on Hari's dates so he wouldn't have to hear him sweet-talk Lila.

Kari felt that Lila was only after their money, which they had carefully saved over the years, believing that in the near future, people would lose their interest in human miracles as technical miracles increased.

Thoughts are like this. They are not on an even line, moving forward like a string pulled taut, but more like a cat's ball of yarn.

As I walk up the stairs behind the man, for example, time seems to slow down. The corridors are white. The steps are polished wood. The molding on the wall has circular designs.

The man stops at a landing. There is a big painting of someone in a uniform and cap. A plaque says the painting is from 1840.

"My great-grandfather," the man says.

"Where's my ma? Is she coming?"

"She's being seen to. Step into my office."

The office is fancy and simple at the same time. There are tall windows without curtains, out of which I can see gray sky, rain, and the tops of a few buildings. "Just let me finish these papers, then you'll have my full attention," he says, his voice smooth as the wood on his furniture. The man is well dressed, but ugly, not like Rhett with his gold hair and blue eyes, his mustache. Where the man should have a chin, he has a flap of fat like a turkey. He shuffles the papers on his desk and lays them out in little piles.

Some people keep bowls of candy or fruit in their office. I search his, but don't see any. If I were rich, I'd have bowls of food everywhere.

I walk to the window and look down at the street. Bodies rushing along. There must be people with real destinations. Or maybe it's just the rain.

An old man comes out of a building with a monkey on his shoulder. The monkey is dressed like the bellman at a fancy hotel. It hops on a wooden Indian in front of a tobacco shop and clutches the Indian's head like a baby would its mother. An apple seller stands on the corner with his big sign: BUY AN APPLE; HELP THE UNEMPLOYED. I imagine that's where Rhett bought my apple. I wish Ma hadn't sent him off this morning.

Slowly, the rain turns white. Snow feels so much better than rain, like something coming, rather than something being washed away. I look up as far as I can, trying to see the moment when it transforms in the sky, water to ice, gray to white.

The man grumbles, wads up a piece of paper, and throws it on the floor. I have a feeling it will not be him who picks it up.

Finally, he turns to me. "I saw you dancing last

night in that grass skirt and I thought, I should take that gal home to my wife."

"I've got a ma already," I say. I have heard of people stealing babies. Ladies who can't have their own. Men, for their wives. Most people aren't interested in stealing older kids, though. Older kids got too much to say, know too much already that can't be unlearned.

"Your daddy got a five-month sentence. You know that, don't you?"

Five months, I think. Nearly half a year. Maybe if I cry, he'll let Pa go. I try to feel something, bring tears to my eyes. I think about Hari and Kari and the bearded lady. If I grew a beard, I'd just pretend to be a man. Then I could do whatever I pleased. I think of Theodore. Is he at home looking out the window too? Then, I imagine Pa being thrown in a dark jail cell, but still, tears won't come.

"Your daddy has taken from people," he continues, "what was not rightly his. He has committed extortion. Do you know what that means? It means he needs to learn a lesson. I'm not a harsh man. I know this will trouble your family. Your mother could be our housekeeper, maybe. How'd you like that?"

I think about it. If they have a nice house, it would be just fine, although I'd end up doing all the work.

But something about the man's eyes make me a little nervous. They jump around the room. And when he talks, his chin wobbles like a warning.

"You can trust me," he says, as if he can read my mind. "I'm a Christian. My family came here on the *Mayflower*. They came here out of faith."

Pa once told me that Jesus was a Jew. He said it was a fact that I should learn to forget.

My empty stomach rises, floats above my eyes. It has forgotten the apple already. Outside, snow gathers on the street in patches.

"You can be Christian," the man says, "and still have something overcome you, like a car might drive into yours and *crash*! Your car will never be the same. Or a tornado touches down on a prairie and wipes a house off the face of this earth. That's how I felt watching you. Do you understand?"

"Are you the mayor?" I ask. Once the mayor of Evanston, Illinois, came to Pa's show. He held out a big key. "This is the key to the city," he said to Pa, but when Pa reached for it, the mayor closed the key into his fist. "Get the message?" the mayor said. And Pa looked like a little kid who'd just dropped his ice cream on the pavement.

"I could buy you a new dress—would you like

that?" The man ignores my question. "I'll bet you'd like one with a fur collar. A pretty girl like you shouldn't have to wear such a ratty dress."

Sometimes, I don't trust talk too much. "I've only had this dress a while," I say.

There is a quick knock at the door. A woman with her hair up on top of her head like a bird's nest comes in and sets a cup of coffee on his desk.

"Watch out for those papers," he scolds, and she moves the cup carefully to the corner of his desk.

"Should I get something for the little girl?" she asks.

"She's not so little."

Again, something has got my tongue. Maybe it's the cat that chased the peacock feather, or the feather itself, tickling the back of my throat so I can't speak. Because what I want to tell the lady is *Yes, get something for the little girl. A chocolate malted or an egg cream. A piece of pie. A cup of coffee, at least.*

My stomach has been kicking up a loud storm since I got here, but the man doesn't seem to notice. No one notices when someone else is hungry, unless they are hungry themselves.

"Don't disturb me again, Rachel," he says. "The sign was up."

The woman backs out of the room.

The man walks over to me. His hands remind me of white fish at the end of his gray sleeves. He bends forward and I think that maybe there's a thread loose on my dress or a bug in my hair, but he just plops his big wet mouth right on my neck and grabs my shoulders with his arms. "Have you ever done this before? I'll bet you have. I'll bet your daddy has lots of ways to make his money."

I push him away and try to run to the door, but he's fast. He catches me halfway across the room and pulls me over toward his desk. He shoves me backward so that my feet fly out from under me. "I saw you last night, half naked up on that rope," he says, leaning the full weight of his body against me. "You were up there teasing all the men, now, weren't you! I'll show you what happens to girls—"

I remember the cup of coffee. I grope behind me with my left arm, but I don't feel it. Then, I swing my right arm back and connect. The hot liquid pours over my hand.

It takes him a moment to figure out what's happened. "Christ!" He releases me. "My papers!"

He runs around the room like the turkey he is, peeling his wet papers apart. "Rachel! Rachel! Damn it!"

"You shouldn't use the Lord's name in vain," I yell

at him, finally finding my voice, like I am some other girl, not one who's been told so many times that she should be seen and not heard.

Rachel rushes in. I think about taking my leave through the door then, but I know that he may be the only one who knows where Ma is.

"I told you not to put the coffee there!" he snaps at her.

"Maybe she'd best wait with me," Rachel says.

"Maybe so," the man hisses, fussing over his precious papers like they were his baby or something.

I follow Rachel into a smaller office.

"I've never seen him so mad. His face was red like a cherry," she whispers. "I thought he'd explode. I was married to a man once who makes this one look like a saint, if you'll believe it. A hunter. That's what my husband was. And nothing made him happier than seeing some nice little bunny hopping along and shooting it. Worst thing was, he didn't even eat meat. He just did it for the fun of it. All the men in that family died before forty. It was a comfort, let me tell you, those ten years of marriage, to know that he wouldn't be alive much longer. He died right on schedule. Now I got me a boyfriend who owns a candy store. Life can get sweeter, honey. It sure can."

Another lady comes in. Behind her is Rhett. I run to him. "The little girl's uncle is here to fetch her."

"How's her mama?"

Rhett nods his head.

"He don't talk," the lady whispers.

"This one barely got away," Rachel tells the lady. "Spilled coffee all over his papers." They both start laughing at that, but Rhett gets that look he has when Pa has yelled at him. He pulls me out the door.

The snow has stopped. The streets are turning mushy and brown. After a big lunch of eggs, hash, fried liver, coconut cake, and lemonade, Rhett and I walk through the town and tear down all our leaflets. Then we head toward the doctor's office, where Ma is resting.

"Do you remember Hari and Kari?" I ask Rhett.

He shakes his head.

"From the carnival? One body. Two heads."

He nods.

"I was just thinking about them today. I wonder if their thoughts got mixed together. Like, are thoughts just in your brain, or do they travel through your blood?"

Rhett frowns at me, his eyes round and blue. He

points to the courthouse, the man's office, as if to say, *What happened*? But I figure we've had trouble enough in this town where luck has gone the way of faith and disappeared.

I shrug, one of his favorite gestures. "It's okay, Rhett. I'm fine."

Rhett hugs me. He shakes his head and I know he knows, and for once I'm glad he can't talk because I don't want to think of the fish man ever again.

Rhett takes my hand. Aside from Hari and Kari, he's the best friend I've ever had.

9

FOR EVERYTHING ITS SEASON,
FOR EVERYTHING UNDER HEAVEN ITS TIME.

—*ECCLESIASTES*

Eventually, Lila Lou dropped Hari and Kari. She said it was because she only liked half of them. Besides, the man with the longest beard in the world promised to take her to Monte Carlo on the next ship. He would shave his beard so it didn't get in his food and she would drink all the water she wanted and they would no longer belong to the "freaks."

"She shrunk away from you," Hari told Kari.

"How does love *shrink*?" Kari argued with him. "If it shrinks, it's not love. Love can only grow."

After Pa goes to jail, Ma and I rent a house in a small town an hour from Detroit. I want Rhett to stay with us, but Ma says he has to go and make money. I cried when I walked with him to the train tracks and waited for one slow enough for him to hop onto. He promised he'd be back soon, making the cross-your-heart gesture so I'd know he really meant it.

It takes the whole twenty-six dollars for six months' rent and a few supplies.

The house is tiny, but at least the roof doesn't leak. Ma thinks it belonged to a sharecropper or a farmhand. There is a room with a wooden floor and a window that looks out on a little valley. There's a woodstove and a sink that doesn't work.

Just outside the door are tall twin elm trees. I like to think they're guarding us.

The toilet is also outside. I have learned not to let my bottom touch the seat because one time it got stuck. It was like putting your tongue on a chunk of ice. We use the Sears catalogue to wipe, which is too bad. It's full of interesting things.

For a week or two, Ma and I just eat things like weeds and old potatoes Ma found in a closet. But then we receive an envelope by mail. The postmark says RHODE ISLAND. After that Ma buys candles, milk, bread, butter, coffee, and even a magazine.

We sit and pore over pictures of Greta Garbo and Jean Harlow. They are dressed so beautifully, it's hard to imagine there's a poor person in the world.

"Who lives in Rhode Island?" I ask Ma.

"Why, *I* did, when I was little," Ma says. "I lived just outside of Providence. You know that!"

Ma tears out a picture of John Barrymore and puts it against the sink, but then she takes it down. "Thou shall have no idols before thee," she sadly tells the actor before she crumples him into a ball and throws him in the fire.

"Do we have family there?"

"Not the likes that want to see me. They didn't take kindly to me running off with your pa, without a proper wedding or anything. Now, why don't you read me something before it gets dark. My eyes are so bad, I can hardly make out the words."

"Who was that letter from?"

"Guess you didn't hear who killed the cat—it was curiosity!"

"Is that where Rhett went?"

"Maybe so. Maybe not."

"How long have you known Rhett?"

"Forever," she says dryly. "Practically."

"Then he must be from Rhode Island too."

"State of Rhode Island and Providence Plantations," Ma says absently. "Big name for such a small state, but it's the prettiest place in the world. There's ocean everywhere."

"I've never seen the ocean."

"That so? No, I guess you haven't." She gets up and straightens the curtains. "I was thinking this spring, maybe you could start school."

"Could I really?"

"There's one still open in the town. Did you know I graduated primary school at the top of my class? I liked geography. You sure do get plenty of that already. After that, my pa said I had to stay home and help my ma."

"Why can't I go to school *now?*" I ask.

"Simple, June: I don't have enough money to dress you properly for winter. You'll start in spring and go until your pa gets out."

"When's he gonna get out?"

"July."

"What did he do wrong?"

"Not a blessed thing. People think that preachers don't have to eat. Think they live on prayers. I've tried that often enough and it don't work."

"But *why* is he in jail?"

"It started as trespassing. That's how it started. That lot was owned by the factory and the foreman didn't take kindly to our presence. But then there was some leftover business from the last time we was in town. A warrant."

"What's extortion?"

"Nothing you need to know about."

"Do you *want* him to come back?"

"Course I do! What a question! Now stop with all this and read to me."

I read aloud from Job. It seems the right book for Pa's circumstances. God allows Satan to take everything from Job. He kills Job's ten children, destroys his home, and gives him boils. Job's friends say it's his fault. He must have done something sinful. Even God can be tempted into a little wager.

"Why are you so keen on that story?" Ma asks.

"I like the way Job's luck changes back," I say.

"Sure, it's great for him. He gets a new set of kids, new animals, and crops. But what about the first wife and kids, who were killed? No one seems to think much about them."

"I guess not."

"God is testing this whole country, if you ask me.

He's up in heaven having a great big party, making a joke of us all."

My mouth just drops open. She is an entirely different person without him—the other Him. "Do you love Pa?"

"When I first saw him preach, I was only sixteen years old. I sang a solo in the choir—'How Great Thou Art.' It was a small church, just one room. The minister gave his sermon every Sunday, and every week half the congregation fell asleep. Then one Sunday, the minister went sick. Your pa was passing through town. Someone heard he was a preacher so they brought him in. Let me tell you that nobody went to sleep with him preaching. When he spoke, it was like thunder and lightning. It was like the whole church was cracked wide open."

"So you fell in love?"

"Who came up with that phrase? *Fall in love.* To fall is usually something bad. Fall down. Fall from grace. Fallen woman."

"Fall leaves," I offer.

"Earlier that day, that very morning, I had prayed for someone to save me. I wanted to go away, to have a life on my own. My parents were farmers. God-fearing people, but it was like all that was between their ears was corn and potatoes, crops and fields. They didn't understand complexities, just right and wrong, black and white. But *I* was complicated. Life was complicated. At least, it had gotten that way. I heard Alfred and I knew that my life had changed. Right after church, he came up to me. To me! To compliment me on my voice. And I realized right away that my prayer had been answered."

"Why did you need to be *saved*?"

"Life is just chapters in a big long book."

"When will Rhett be back?"

Ma looks at the window as if she expects to see him. "Don't know."

"Was it him that sent that money?"

"Keep reading."

"I know it was."

"I'm not saying it was or it wasn't."

"Why are you always so mad at Rhett?"

"He disappointed me once, that's all. Come to think of it, you're the only person who hasn't disappointed me."

"I never will, Ma."

"I know."

When the fire burns low, we lie down next to the stove. I recite the rest of Job from memory. I know most of the Bible by heart, even the deadly boring Leviticus. Pa's been having me recite it ever since I can remember. He says it will prepare me for my life as a lady preacher. It's the only book I've ever read. "'. . . *For there is hope for a tree,*'" I recite. "'*If it is cut down, that it will sprout again, and that its shoots will not cease. Though its root grows old in the earth and its stump dies in the ground, yet at the scent of water it will bud and put forth branches like a young plant. . . .*'"

I hear Ma's slow breath, but it doesn't seem fair somehow, her sleeping when I'll be up half the night watching the sky press against the window.

"Ma?"

"Huh?"

"I don't want to be a preacher."

I peer out the window. A long rope is tied between two trees, a clothesline that we haven't used because the air is too cold to dry clothes outside. I can see myself perched on it in one of my costumes, like some kind of trained parrot.

Since we've been here, I haven't practiced once.

10

AM I MY BROTHER'S KEEPER?
—*Cain answering God*, GENESIS

Spring finally comes. The landscape cracks open. The square hedges burst free from their tight forms. Heavy with leaves, the twin elms lean close enough to touch each other.

Pa was a twin. He and his brother were identical. When they were born, my grandpa wanted to name them Esau and Jacob, like the twins in the Bible. But my grandma said no, because Esau and Jacob never got along. Esau was the firstborn and Jacob came out second, clutching Esau's heel. It was a gesture that was continued throughout their life: Jacob dogging Esau, making sure he wouldn't get ahead of him. Jacob even talked Esau into selling him his birthright in exchange for a bowl of red lentils.

My grandma named them Alfred and Abraham: two A's like two peas in a pod, she thought, the first letters of the alphabet. The first. At least that's how it was told. She died shortly after.

Like Cain and Abel, Esau and Jacob, Joseph and his brothers, Pa and Abraham never really got along.

"It was Abraham's head that killed my mother," Pa once told me. "It was too big. He 'bout tore her to pieces and she never healed up. And he stayed big-headed, in every way."

Since it's warmer, Ma goes more frequently to visit Pa at the prison. She says I'm not allowed to come because the inmates swear too much.

Now that the room is not so cold and her hands can move better, Ma begins to sew. She sews a quilt for a lady in town and earns fifty cents. With the scraps, she sews a bedspread for me and a pillowcase with an embroidered sunflower. At night, I lay my head on its center, the petals like melted butter.

A rich lady in town hires Ma to help around her house. Ma comes back and talks about the scent of furniture polish on cherry wood and the way white lace can be made into doilies and placed onto tables just to look pretty. Ma seems younger somehow, softer, now that she has a warm bed, food, and work. Sometimes, she even smiles.

One Sunday morning, just after Ma and I have said our prayers, Rhett appears. He sets his stuff down in the corner of the kitchen and sits at the table like he's never been away. His hair is cut short and he is wearing new clothes.

"Rhett, you shaved your mustache." I hug him.

"Look what the cat has dragged in," Ma barks, pouring a cup of coffee and setting it out at the table. "Do you have a house?"

Rhett shakes his head.

"Well, you best sleep in the car."

He shrugs.

"Drink it quickly," she bosses. "We've got to lay out a garden."

I sit on Rhett's lap to make up for Ma's meanness. He gives me a sack of candied almonds and a little doll with blond hair and blue eyes like mine. He makes a sign that means, *Missed you.*

In the afternoon, the three of us hoe the ground, which feels like there's still a sheet of ice beneath the surface. Ma keeps being mean to Rhett, but I can tell she's happy that he's here. "We grew tomatoes in the summer when I was little. Remember those? They tasted like they were made of sugar," she says to him. "We had plenty of food then. We gave the leftovers to the pigs."

He nods and makes a gesture that I don't understand, but Ma says, "Oh yes. That was a feast, and then the hayride . . ."

By evening, our plot has finally been dug up. I make a pot of soup with bacon and beans, while Ma and Rhett decide what to plant. When I go to the door to call them for supper, I see a rare sight: Ma leaning against her hoe, laughing.

The next morning, I get to start school. Ma and Rhett argue for an hour because Rhett wants to come along.

"What'll folks think of me showing up with you?" Ma says.

Rhett draws a circle around us with his hand. *They'll think we're a family.* He puts his hat on and walks behind us.

"He would never be so impertinent if your pa were here," Ma says to me.

By the time we get to the schoolhouse, Rhett has caught up with us. He holds the door open for Ma.

"You're impossible," she hisses at him. He grins back at her.

The teacher who comes to meet us is the prettiest lady I've ever seen. She has long brown hair tied behind her back like the tail of a chestnut mare. Her name is Miss O'Doul. She speaks with an accent and tells us she's from Ireland. Because of hard times, there are only two teachers left in the school. Many ages are mixed together and the classes are big.

"Now, I'll take care of her. Don't you two worry," Miss O'Doul says as she leads me away from Ma and Rhett.

"She's a good girl," Ma says, which makes me happy. It is the first time she has ever said so.

When we reach the door to the classroom, Miss O'Doul turns and gives a final wave to Rhett and Ma. Then she smiles her pretty smile at me. "My goodness," she says. "You're the spitting image of your father."

II

ASK, AND IT WILL BE GIVEN TO YOU;
SEEK AND YOU SHALL FIND.
KNOCK AND THE DOOR WILL BE OPENED.

—*BOOK OF MATTHEW*

I've been thinking a lot lately about Jesus' Sermon on the Mount. Pa likes the bit about not casting pearls before swine. That's what he goes on about when we don't get much in the collection box.

Ma likes the part about asking and it will be given to you. For years, she's been praying for a church where Pa could work. Her longing could drive a flock of sheep off a cliff, but it has never come to pass.

I like the advice about seeking and finding. I have been seeking for answers my whole life, it seems, about how life can be so hard for some and easy for others, and about how to know God when He seems so far away sometimes.

Jesus talks about a lot of other things in his Sermon on the Mount that people still remember. I guess it's easier to get people to listen when you're standing above them. Maybe that's why Pa has such a hard time. He is down on the ground, while I'm the one way up high.

Miss O'Doul introduces me to the class. I look around the room for a smile or a friendly face, but the way the kids stare at me I might as well have two heads like Hari and Kari.

The classroom is crowded. There are wooden tables and benches, the kids shoved in next to each other. As Miss O'Doul leads me to my seat, everyone watches and whispers erupt like bubbles on a stream. I don't catch it all, but someone says something about the ugliness of my dress. Someone else comments on my hair.

Finally, I squeeze between two kids. Miss O'Doul introduces me to them. On one side is a girl with hair the color of fresh strawberries. Her name is Sara. On the other side is a boy named Gus who has brown hair and big ears. When he hands me a little board, I ask him what I do with it. He laughs so hard his big ears wiggle and he yells, "Miss O'Doul, she don't even know what a slate is!"

"Quiet down," Miss O'Doul scolds. "I will now read the news, which is no laughing matter." The class turns toward her, their eyes serious again, as she reads about a family freezing to death right in their own house and a demonstration in Washington, D.C., where police killed seven factory workers and jailed fifty more. It makes me think about Pa, in jail for five months. I try to picture him there, but for some reason, I can't remember his face.

When I was little, before I got Pa's interest by being in his show, it was always his legs I encountered: his trousers, tweedy and scratchy against my skin; his muddy shoes. One time a man punched Pa and knocked him down. I remember this because when he was lying on his back, I ran over to him and was surprised to find that his whiskers had become gray.

Once I started walking the rope, though, Pa talked to me all the time. He put his face right up to mine as he instructed me. He recited scripture for me to memorize. And he told me stories of when he was a boy, how he sat up in a tree for three days, waiting for the voice of God, thinking it would sound like thunder, and then being surprised to find it came to him as just a rustle of leaves. Then silence.

He told me about his brother Abraham, how he could speak like a politician, smooth words and fancy speeches dropping from his mouth like it was nothing.

When Pa was little, he said, he kept having the same dream that he was lost in the woods. Then his mother's face, white with death, would appear among the trees and she would whisper suggestions to him about how to find his way, but so softly, he couldn't make out the words.

Miss O'Doul has us recite the capitals of states, then she talks about the economy of Europe, and the structure of our government. I think that maybe this *is* the way to seek, because facts stay in your body forever. They don't disappear like a big meal you have eaten in the morning, only to be hungry again at noon, or like rain hitting the hot ground and evaporating in an instant.

The last thing we do is addition and subtraction, using small colored pebbles. It makes me think about the Old and New Testament. The Old Testament is about addition. God shows favor by adding land, wives, fruit, wine, mistresses, and children. Be fruitful

and multiply. But the New Testament is about subtraction. Jesus and the apostles shed their lives, possessions, and families. I share this with Miss O'Doul
when she comes to check my sums. "That's very
insightful, June." She strokes my hair. "And your sums
are just perfect. Jolly for you."

"My ma taught me," I tell her.

After school, Ma has said for me to walk straight
home, but the other kids are standing around, talking
and opening up their lunch pails to see what's left
inside.

No one says anything to me. Even Sara is busy
giggling in a circle of girls.

I start to walk home, but then I notice a wall along
the schoolyard. It is rocky on the sides, but flat and
smooth on the top.

The wall is a lot wider than a rope, so it's easy to
balance. I start with a series of cartwheels. Then I flip
in the air.

Sara stops talking to her friends and walks
over. Then some more kids come. Soon, everyone is
watching.

"Will you look at that?"

"How does she do it?"

"I wanna try."

When I jump down, the kids gather around me in a circle. Gus seems to have forgotten about the slate. "Which way do you live, June?" he says.

I point.

"Well, I'll walk you then."

"I live that way, so *I'm* walking her home," a boy with blond hair interrupts.

"No chance, Macon," Gus argues.

"She doesn't want to go with boys, so *I'll* take her home." Sara loops her arm in mine and together we march off, with Gus and Macon trailing behind.

12

FOR NOW WINTER IS PAST
THE RAINS ARE OVER AND GONE
THE FLOWERS APPEAR IN THE COUNTRYSIDE.
— *Song of Solomon*

In his Sermon on the Mount, Jesus talks about a lot of different things. He talks about entering heaven through the narrow gate. When I was little, I thought that meant only thin people got in.

He talks about how blessed are the hungry, the suffering, the meek, and the poor. There sure are a lot of blessed people around these days. Let's hope the gate has gotten wider.

After his sermon, Jesus comes down among the throngs and heals people left and right. He heals a leper whose skin has rotted, half his nose dropped off. He cures the blind, the sick, brings back the dead, all the while preaching, weaving a cloth of stories that illustrate the will of God.

Of course, Jesus is a lot more somber when He's being crucified—less self-assured. He preached on a mountain, performed miracles, overturned the tables of the moneylenders, spent forty days and nights being tempted by the devil. But nothing prepared him for the torture and humiliation of the crucifixion. "Father," he cries out. "Why have you forsaken me?"

But God hasn't forsaken Jesus after all. After a slow death and a funeral, Jesus is yanked right up into heaven.

As Easter approaches, everything comes into bloom. The hedges break out of their square forms. Roses burst wildly from thorny skeletons. Gus, Sara, Macon, and I spend each afternoon together, doing what we please.

"Look at the four of them," Miss O'Doul says to the other teacher as we march through the hall, "as thick as thieves."

We like the sound of that, so we create a game called Thieves. Two of us set up a treasure and the other two have to try to steal it. It might be a chain of daisies, or food, or a painted rock from Macon's garden.

Gus and I climb the crab apple tree and hide four acorns in an old bird's nest. Sara and Macon hide cookies on a little island in the middle of a pond. By the time we find them, the cookies are soaking wet.

Sometimes we even sneak onto one of the few big farms that have survived these hard times. One of them is owned by old Mr. Shepherd. It has cornfields, horses, sheep, cows, and pigs. Gus and Macon say Mr. Shepherd murdered his whole family with an ax and he keeps their heads in the cellar of his house. But Sara says his wife just ran off from him, along with their five kids.

We make a game of running through his field to the house. We go in teams of two just in case Shepherd comes after us with his ax, which Macon says glimmers like "a moonlit razor."

Other times, we just walk around after school or sit in the library, where we discuss the important things in life. We might talk about the things we learned in school, like how to divide a pie into enough pieces to feed a certain number of people. Or how important timber is to the economy of central Europe, or what to expect from a new German leader named Hitler.

Then, Easter Sunday, we have a festival at the

school. Ma sews a new shirt for Rhett and matching dresses with embroidered flowers for her and me. People have taken to the notion that Rhett is my pa. Given our circumstances, Ma says, it's best not to correct them. It keeps the women folks from talking and the men from "molesting" us, although I haven't seen any inclined in that direction. Besides, as soon as Pa shows up, he will make us leave. So it doesn't matter. Even though we have a house, food, work, and friends. He will make us leave.

Rhett, Ma, and I walk to the school in the sunshine, feeling like we don't have a care in the world. The air is scented with roses, honeysuckle, and lilac. The sky is so blue and bright it is impossible to imagine Jesus sweaty and forlorn on a cross between two thieves, but easy to envision his resurrection.

Miss O'Doul has made an egg hunt for the little kids and Sara's ma has brought dyed eggs and sugar cookies. Macon has written an Easter play that we perform for everyone. I play Mary Magdalene because of my gold hair, which Macon says makes me look like a fallen woman put straight again. Sara plays mother Mary and Gus plays the dead Jesus. At first Gus was mad because all he does the whole play is lie under a sheet, but then he found out he got to fly.

The play goes pretty well, but when two boys pull the rope for Gus to rise to heaven, they yank so hard that he flies across the room with the shroud still on him, looking everything like a ghost.

It's supposed to be the solemn moment, but the audience can't help themselves. They roar with laughter. Even Ma holds her handkerchief in front of her face so no one will see her smile.

The play ends. The audience applauds. As we take our bows, I see something that makes my jaw drop open: Rhett turns to Ma, puts his arm around her, and kisses her right on the mouth. And she lets him.

13

HOW DULL IS THE GOLD
HOW TARNISHED THE FINE GOLD.

—LAMENTATIONS

I will never get used to the way things end and how they never start up again once they're finished. At least for me who is always moving and moving.

The last day of school, I can't swallow. It's like there's a big rock in my throat. Miss O'Doul talks about her summer, how she'll visit her parents in Ireland and see her new baby niece. As we leave, she passes out gifts to all the kids: boxes of chalk, packages of gum, apples, and toys.

I want to tell her that she's the smartest person in the world and that the hours in her class were the happiest of my life, but when I open my mouth, no sound comes out. It's like in dreams I've had where Pa pushes me onto a stage, all dressed in white like Aimee Semple McPherson, and I'm supposed to preach. I gaze at the crowd, planning to talk about Solomon, how when two women claim to be mother of the same baby, he offers to cut the baby in half. Then one woman cries out, "No! Give the baby to the other," and Solomon knows she's the mother. In the dream, I open my mouth, but no words will come.

"What is it, June? You've been my very best student, truth be told. This is for you." Miss O'Doul gives me a book.

I stumble out onto the lawn, grasping my book, blinded by the river in my eyes and the bright summer light.

"There she is." I hear Macon's voice. "Come on, June. We're free!"

"Wake up!" Gus socks me.

"What did Miss O'Doul give to you?" Sara asks.

I hold up the book.

"*Grimms' Fairy Tales*," Macon reads.

"I always said you were Miss O'Doul's favorite. Didn't I say that, Sara?" Gus says.

"Yes, Gus, you always said that." Sara sounds mad.

"What did you get, Sara?" I find my voice.

"A hair ribbon." Sara holds up a pretty blue ribbon with white lace trim, perfect for her orange hair.

"I got a ruler," Macon says.

"I think the hair ribbon's the nicest," I lie.

"You didn't see mine." Gus pulls out a little plastic pig with jaws that open and shut. "Now, why do you suppose she gave me that?"

"I had a real cow," Macon says. "It said 'Noo' instead of 'Moo.' It probably knew it would get slaughtered."

"I had a mynah bird," Sara chimes in. "He talked, but my aunt went to wash the cage and set the bird on the clothesline and he just flew away. A week later my neighbor heard his voice coming from the trees. But we never caught him."

They discuss what might have happened to the talking bird that was only used to living in cages. Then I follow, still choked with sadness, while they set out to Shepherd's farm to listen to his animals. "Maybe they're talking about those heads in the cellar," Gus says, "but nobody's bothered to listen."

"There's no heads in the cellar," Sara argues.

"I saw them, through the window, all of them. The heads were cut off and the eyes were gouged out and blood was pouring from the mouths."

"You're lying," Sara says.

"He is not," Macon replies. "Go see for yourself."

That evening, just before dark, we watch Mr. Shepherd drive off in his truck. Then Sara and I crawl along on our hands and knees until we get to the cellar window.

"Should we break the window?" I ask.

"No. Someone might hear. I know," Sara says. "Let's just say we went in there and didn't see anything. They won't know the difference."

"Who won't know the difference?" comes a loud, deep voice. Sara screams.

"Booo!" Gus and Macon jump out from behind a bush.

Sara socks Macon. "You scared me to death."

"Shhh." I press against the window. It swings open inside. "Lower me in," I tell Macon and Gus.

The drop to the floor isn't far. But once inside, it's pitch dark. A smell that might or might not be dead bodies makes me feel sick. "I need a match."

"I got one." Macon drops in after me. "P.U., it stinks."

"Are the heads there?" Sara calls out.

"It sure smells like it," Macon says. He lights a

match. In the corner of the room, the heads come
into view.

"There they are," I whisper. Sara squeals. The
match goes out.

"Here's a lantern," Gus drops in. "I don't know if
there's oil in it."

Macon lights the lantern. "The heads are . . ."

"Cabbages!" I exclaim. Six rotting cabbages—
shrunken, fruit fly–infested, oozing, blackened leaves
peeling like skin—line the wall of the cellar.

"Ugh, I'm gonna puke," Gus says. "It's *worse* than
cutoff heads."

"Let's get out of here," Macon says. "They stink."

"Farmer Shepherd's coming!" Sara whispers. "Hurry."

His tires screech on the gravel road.

Macon and Gus hoist me up. Then Sara and I yank
them up by their arms. "Run!"

The lights from his truck swing toward us as we
dash into the cornfield.

"What are we running for anyway?" Gus pants.
He looks as deflated as the cabbages. "He didn't even
kill 'em."

"Yeah." Sara stops. "He's as harmless as a flea."

"You never know," I say to make Gus feel better.
"He could've killed them and buried them."

"Or maybe he caught on to us and smuggled the heads out," Macon adds.

"You think?" Gus asks.

"Now he's seen us," I say.

"I hope he doesn't tell my mother," Sara whines.

But Gus peps up. "I'm telling you. Kids have disappeared around his place and no one has ever seen them again."

"I heard about that," I lie. "Two girls and two boys."

"Really?" Sara says.

"Just like us."

"Yeah," Macon agrees. "I heard that too. Watch out for his blade when you sleep. Next time, it could be us."

When I get home and hear crashing sounds inside, the first thing I think of is Farmer Shepherd. But as I peer through the window, I just see Ma. She is standing next to the stove, throwing anything she can get her hands on: pots, pans, even the dish towel hanging on the sink. Tears run down her face and her hair is wild, like someone possessed by the devil. "Oh." She sees me and drops her hands.

"I'm sorry I got home late," I say.

"He's gone again," Ma says.

"Rhett?"

"Who else?"

I look into the corner where Rhett kept his few things. It's empty.

"I just felt like throwing a few things," Ma says with a sigh, bending over to pick up a pan.

"He'll be back," I say, but I must admit I feel pretty downhearted too. The last couple of months, we'd been like a real family.

I WENT DOWN TO THE NUT ORCHARD,
TO LOOK AT THE BLOSSOMS OF THE VALLEY,
TO SEE WHETHER THE VINES HAD BUDDED,
WHETHER THE POMEGRANATES WERE IN BLOOM.
— *Song of Solomon*

Animals talk in the fairy tales too. My favorite is about a flounder who grants a fisherman a wish for his wife. But the fisherman's wife is greedy. First she asks for a new house, then a mansion, then to be an empress, then a god. Nothing satisfies her, so the flounder takes everything away and she is poor again.

Another one I love is about the twelve brothers who are turned into ravens and can only be saved if their sister is silent for seven years. Because she won't speak, she is tied to a stake to be burned to death. Just then, the seven years finally pass and her brothers arrive to save her.

Girls in fairy tales are very patient.

If Ma gets home early enough from her work at the lady's house, I read to her from my new book. It gives us a nice change from Job and Isaiah.

Much to my surprise, Ma is familiar with the stories. "I remember that one from when I was little," she says.

Ma's memory of her childhood is like one of those globes that you shake and a beautiful snowy scene appears. For a second, everything is perfect.

Many of the fairy tales have lessons that remind me of when *I* was little, before Pa took charge of me. Back then, Ma used to tell me teaching stories, about a boy who stuck his finger in a dike, a boy who cried wolf, or a girl who disobeyed her father and was sent into the woods. Ma would speak in proverbs. *Haste makes waste,* she'd say. Or, *God helps he who helps himself.*

Today, when I tell her how sad I am about school being over, she only says, "*Time heals.*"

But in this case, the reverse is true. Ma has pasted a calendar to the wall and there she marks off the days until Pa is released.

I try not to look at it.

Time wounds.

Instead, I read, carry water to the plants, sweep

the floor, and wash clothes, while Ma goes to work at the lady's house. If Ma leaves a quarter, I buy milk, sugar, flour, and cornmeal. Sometimes I buy bacon or chicken. Then I meet Sara, Macon, and Gus at the river, newly flushed from a big rain.

We sit on the big flat stones and eat a picnic Sara's ma has packed and talk about what will happen when we grow up, which seems so far away and close at the same time. Sara says she'll get married. Macon says he'll study law or be a soldier if there's ever another war and Gus wants to be a farmer. When the bank repossessed his parents' farm, they tried to auction it. Then the other farmers came with clubs, hammers, and hoes. When anyone tried to bid on his farm, the other farmers hit their weapons on the ground. Finally, the bank had to sell the farm back to Gus's pa for less than he owed.

The story makes me think of the Salvation Army people talking about the workers "organizing." America may be a sinking ship, like Ma says, but at least some people are trying to swim.

"June never says what she wants to be," Macon prompts, his white blond hair falling down over his eyes.

I consider the women in the Bible who have good

and interesting lives. There aren't very many of them. A lot of them are raped, cast out, killed, or are servants who have to just work and have babies for the master. Even more are just wives who follow after their husbands and try to keep quiet. But there are exceptions.

There's Queen Esther, who marries the stupid King Ahasuerus and creates a plan to save the Jewish people. There's Deborah, who gets to fight in the battlefield. And there's Ruth, who chooses to remain loyal to her mother-in-law, Naomi, and of course, Mary Magdalene, who follows Jesus.

"Well?"

"I just want to stay here," I say.

"But what do you want to *be*?" Sara asks.

I think hard about this. When I tell Ma I don't want to be a preacher, she acts like she doesn't hear me.

If not a preacher, then what? *Teacher,* I want to say, but it seems too far away, too impossible.

"I'll bet you wanna marry some rich man and live in New York in a big fancy house," Gus says, peeling a scab on his knee.

"I think we should marry each other, then live as next-door neighbors," Sara says, peering at Macon.

"I'll marry June," Gus and Macon say at the same time.

"I have a better idea." I throw my arm around Sara's shoulder. "Sara and I will live together and keep a nice tidy house, then you two messy boys can live next door to us."

"Who says we're messy?" Gus argues, his face covered with dirt, his hair sticking up every which way.

"I like June's idea," Sara says, still miffed at their insult. "Who wants to live with dirty boys."

"Okay, fine. Gus and I will live together," Macon says.

"Deal," I say.

"Deal."

"Spit in your hand," Gus says solemnly.

"Why?" Ma has always told me that spitting is impolite.

"Just do it!"

The four of us spit in our hands.

"Now swear!" Gus says.

"What should we swear to?" I ask.

"That we'll do what we said we'd do in our lives."

Sara, always the practical one, says, "What if we change our minds?"

"I know!" Macon says. "Let's swear that no matter what we do, we'll never be apart."

"Swear," they all say.

We all rub our hands together.

"June didn't swear."

"I swear," I say, and in that moment I am so swept away by faith that I believe, I almost do, that I'll be here with them forever.

15

IF YOU WANT GOD TO LAUGH, TELL HIM YOUR PLAN.
— *Old saying*

There's something that's always stumped me about Abraham. When God wants to destroy Sodom and Gomorrah and kill all the people there, Abraham is brave and argues with God: "Will you indeed sweep away the righteous with the wicked? Suppose there are fifty righteous within the city; will you then sweep away the place and not forgive it for the fifty righteous who are in it?"

God says He won't destroy the town if there are fifty righteous people in it. Then Abraham keeps on arguing, bringing the number, slowly, down to one. God says that even for one, He will not destroy the place.

Yet when it comes to God telling Abraham to sacrifice his own son Isaac, Abraham just brings Isaac on up the mountain and prepares to slaughter him! He doesn't argue one bit.

At supper time, we four "thieves" scatter to our separate houses. I race straight up the hill, bringing dandelion greens for Ma to cook up like she does with bacon and sugar. The door is wide open, a rectangle of dark in the waning light. Ma never leaves the door open, concerned as she is about being "molested." It stops me cold.

I can recognize Pa's voice anywhere. It's like a fiddle with the strings stretched taut. And when I hear it, I think about running far into the fields or hiding in Mr. Shepherd's cellar with all those rotting black cabbages, those heads that were and then were not the dead members of his family.

How should I be? That's a question I often ask myself, when there is some long road between the way I'm supposed to behave and the way I feel.

How should I be with Pa?

I drop the greens and wait at the door without him noticing me.

Ma is pacing back and forth in front of the stove.

"It's just . . . they should tell a man's wife if he's going to be released is all. Then, I'd have met you there."

"You want me to go back, so you can see me out properly?" Pa hisses.

"Don't be silly."

Despite Abraham's arguments, Sodom and Gomorrah are eventually destroyed because there aren't any righteous people there except Lot, who gets to leave. I've often wondered why Lot's wife wasn't counted as one of the righteous people. That would have made it at least two. I guess only the men were counted. Lot's wife doesn't make out too well. She looks back, just like I do when I'm leaving a place, and is turned into a pillar of salt. And Abraham doesn't have to kill Isaac after all. It turns out, God was only joking.

Pa starts to roll a cigarette, but then he stops and looks straight at me. It's like he's known I'm there all along. "Cat got your tongue, June?"

"Hey, Pa," I croak.

"Grown tall, June. Even gotten a little fat, haven't ya?"

"How was prison?" I ask stupidly.

"Just fine, if you like to be kept in a cage and eat

slop not fit for pigs. If you like to hear stories and language that'll make ya feel you've fallen into the bowels of hell. My own crown of thorns. But at least I saved one hundred souls."

"A hundred souls!" Ma tries to sound excited. "Did you hear that, June?"

"One hundred souls," Pa says again, but his voice sounds dull, like a key on a piano that hasn't been tuned for a long time.

"Jesus was nailed next to a thief," Ma adds, as if there's some connection.

Pa cracks his knuckles one by one. He lifts up objects on the table and puts them down: a mug, a plate, a pincushion Ma embroidered. He walks to the window and peers out at the sunflowers, carrots, green beans, and tomatoes. "Who helped you with that garden?"

"Uhm . . ." Ma looks over at me, and I can see she's trying to decide whether to talk about Rhett or not. I think about the way Rhett kissed her at the play, the nights we've sat together eating like a regular family.

"I did," I say.

"Have you been practicing, June? With all the gardening you've been doing?" He looks at Ma. "Has she?"

Ma tugs at a button on her shirt; it comes off in her

hand. A bug crawls slowly along the floor. It is black and shiny. I can almost hear its hair-thin legs scratching the wooden planks.

Ma stares at the button. "Now, where did this come from?"

"I don't see a rope."

"I practiced some," I say, swallowing the lie by thinking about the times I've climbed on tree branches, leaped stone to stone in the river, the day I won them over with my performance at school.

"Can't wait to get out of this state." Pa smashes the bug under his shoe. "I'd leave this second, but it's too dark to check out the car. Where's Rhett?"

"Here's your coffee." Ma sets the cup down hard. Coffee spills over the rim onto the table, but she doesn't mop it up.

"I'm sure he's around, now, isn't he?"

"The car's out back," Ma says.

"Did you at least start the engine while I've been gone?"

"Alfred. If you'd a wanted me to start the engine you should'a told me one of the times when I was visiting you."

"You can't expect me to think of everything, can you?"

"No. Well, 'course not. But I've had my hands full with June. The girl don't know what to do with herself without you here."

I give Ma a dirty look: What she said is an out-and-out lie. My only problem is there's too much I want to do with myself and not enough hours in the day.

"Well, then?" Pa stands. "Pack up!"

He's down to just jangling bones. Pa looks like a puppet more than ever. Who's pulling his strings?

He sure is pulling ours.

16

HONOR THY MOTHER AND THY FATHER.

—The fifth commandment

Like Abraham, Moses squabbles with God plenty. When God turns Moses' sister Miriam into a leper because she said mean things about Moses' wife, he chides God: "I have forgiven her, why can't you?"

And when God is mad at the Jews for being scared to enter Egypt, Moses begs God to be patient with them.

This is something I admire about Moses. It takes a lot of courage to argue with your creator.

As if summer has met with a sudden death, the next morning sweeps in a strange winter cold. Rhett sweeps in too.

Jesus tells the apostles to shed their lives and follow him. When a disciple asks to bury his father first, Jesus says, "Let the dead bury the dead." I never understood why Jesus couldn't just wait for him to put his father in the ground. He directs Matthew to leave his tax booth, others to leave their fishing boats, their wives and children, their lives.

What has Rhett shed to follow us?

"I have not come to bring peace," Jesus said, "but a sword."

Maybe that explains something.

"You knew Pa was being released early?" I follow Rhett outside to the car.

He sets the suitcases down and looks at me. He nods yes. Then he takes off his scarf and wraps it around my neck. My eyes smart with tears. "Can't you do something, Rhett?" I beg. "I don't want to go. . . ."

Instead of the shrug I expect, Rhett puts his hands on my shoulders and stares at me. He opens his mouth and his lips move like he is about to speak.

"Get those suitcases into the car, Rhett," Pa commands. "June, get into the back!"

I climb into the car. Pa leans inside. His breath smells like pennies, coffee, and smoke. "You're not embarrassed that your old man was in jail, are you?"

"No." Embarrassment is not what I'm feeling. What I'm feeling is just how much I'd like to see him back in jail, even if it isn't "fit for pigs."

"We'll get this show back on the road, then."

This time, when we pull away, I don't look back. There are no aunts or uncles or grandparents in my imaginings to wave to and who'll wish for our return. There are only real people: Sara, Macon, and Gus, and I didn't get to say good-bye.

Rhett pats my hand, then squeezes it. "Do something," I whisper. "You should." These are the words I say to Rhett, but even I don't know what it is he *should do*.

In the car, hour after hour, I keep myself from being sad by reading Miss O'Doul's book. In fairy tales, it's usually the women who are wicked, like the mother in *Hansel and Gretel* who'd rather see her children be eaten by wild animals than share her food, or the witch in the candy house who plans to eat them. There are wicked enchantresses and witches, horrible stepmothers and stepsisters. They are powerful women, but mean.

At least in fairy tales, girls are usually the main character, unlike in the Bible. Like Cinderella, who has to clean ashes, and her sisters, who have their eyes pecked out by birds. Or Briar Rose, who is put into a long silent sleep. In the end, if the girls are lucky, they get to marry some king, live in a castle, eat feasts, and get fat.

I like to imagine myself in the stories. I am in a tower spinning straw into gold or in a castle cleaning through ashes. I am lost in the woods. But then Pa starts popping up in my imaginings. He is also trapped among the trees, wandering and wandering, dropping bread crumbs to find his way, which the birds promptly eat up. He becomes lost, hungry. A witch comes to turn him into some object, a crumbling stone tower, a tree, a toad that has to sleep in the water for a hundred years before someone bothers to kiss him and set him free.

Usually Ma chatters when we're driving. Since we left, though, she's been absolutely silent. Maybe she's thinking about our garden, the tomatoes and green beans that will wither on the vine, or maybe she's thinking about Rhett, silent in the backseat, how she kissed him and won't get a chance to ever again.

As if to fill the air, Pa says, "You wouldn't guess who was a prison guard, Agnes."

"Who?"

"Big Ben."

"Why didn't you tell me?" Ma asks. "I could've said hello to him on one of my visits."

"There weren't many visits, now were there? Besides, I'm telling you now."

It's hard to imagine Big Ben working as a guard. He was so small and scared of everything. Pa often tells the crowd that God is mighty, with fire in one hand and a sword in the other. Then God sounds a bit like a prison guard.

"How ever did he get to work at a prison in Detroit? *He* didn't end up in jail, did he?"

"Now why would one of *your* illustrious family members end up in jail? Just your husband! Besides, they don't make prisoners into jailers. Think, once in a while, Agnes."

Rhett clenches and unclenches his fists. I pull part of my blanket over him so he won't feel so mad.

"Well, I'm sorry. I was just worrying that Big Ben took a wrong turn," Ma says.

"You mean like *me*."

"I mean," she says hurriedly, "it's not like *everyone's* in jail by mistake. I thought he wanted to work on cars."

"When he was done with that fool business of

running away from home," Pa says, "he went back, but his ma had died."

"Alice died? Oh, no."

"He went into town and took an apprenticeship with a mechanic, but he didn't have a talent for working on cars. He mixed up the parts. He was hardly a brain, was he?"

"Alice was still young." Ma buries her face in her hands.

"Well, there's no use crying over spilt milk. Anyway, Big Ben is doing all right now. He's a prison guard and he's going to get married to a sister of one of the murderers there."

Aside from preaching, it's the first time I've heard Pa string together so many sentences. "String together" is something Miss O'Doul said about words. She said words were pearls and sentences were necklaces. You had to string those pearls just so to make a nice necklace.

"You hear all that about Big Ben, June? June always liked Big Ben." Ma wipes her face.

"June likes everyone," Pa replies, as if liking people is a bad thing. He turns and looks at me. "Isn't that right?" A big plop of bird mess splatters the windshield. I don't say anything. The bird has already expressed my sentiments. "What's that book you're reading, June? It's not the Bible."

"Huh?"

"I said . . . what are you reading?"

"*Grimms' Fairy Tales*. Miss O'Doul gave it to me at the end of the year."

"So Miss O'Doul was a teacher. Is that right?"

"She's the smartest person I ever met," I brag. Somehow, though, I get the feeling I've said the wrong thing.

"I don't remember you mentioning *school* on any of your visits, Agnes."

"I'm sure I did, Alfred. Of course I did. I was working and the child needed to stay out of trouble."

"*Working*. And you didn't save a dime."

"We had to live."

"And what does that book say, June?" Pa asks.

"Say?"

"Read it to me. Right there, where you are."

"Why?"

"Just do it!"

"So the servant ate the white snake," I read. "And no sooner had he, than he could understand the language of the forest, and all the animals' speech in the world—"

The car swerves as Pa turns, yanks the book from my hand, and throws it out the window. "Paganism!" he says. "Pure and simple. Sounds like the blasted Book of Mormon!"

"My book!"

"Now it's just a bird, flying away."

"Why are you so afraid to have her learn something?" Ma says, louder than I've ever heard her.

"Guess you've forgotten something, Agnes. Guess you've forgotten that I'm the man of the house. Anytime you want, you can just stop coming along with us. Me and June can do without you."

The idea of going along with just Pa, and not Ma, makes me chilled down to my bones. I start to shiver. Rhett pulls me closer. Something about his heavy arm loosens all the tears inside of me, like two rivers carving out the earth of my skin.

17

For as long as I can remember, Pa thinks folks are out to do him harm. I guess, judging from what happened to him in Michigan, he has good reason.

His life story, what little he's told me, seems pretty sad. "My pa was the best preacher ever," Pa told me once, when I was practicing. "He believed that there were only *some* folks elected to walk God's path. I believe that *anyone* can go to heaven if they're willing to sacrifice themselves on earth."

"Did he think he was one of the chosen ones?"

"Of course. But he didn't think *I* was. This mark I've had on my shoulder since birth . . . he said it was the devil's mark and no matter how many times he tried to burn it off, it didn't go away. It just got darker."

"Did your brother have that mark too?"

"Abraham?" Pa spit on the ground. "Nah. It was the one physical difference between us, that and his big head."

"What happened to your pa? Is he still alive?"

"Nope."

"When did he die?"

"Twenty years ago or so. In Utah. He was stoned to death."

"Why?"

"For being a heretic, for speaking the word about God's wrath and Revelations. The world would end soon, he told the people, in fire, in ice, in locusts swarming down to devour the harvests, in crows turning on crowds and plucking out their eyes. Then Christ would rise up on an oyster shell. Christ would be the pearl, he told them. And the lot of them would burn in eternal flames for their wickedness, their skin bubbling and boiling like Job's."

"How terrible."

"Not at all. It's the kind of death he would've wanted."

I wonder what kind of death our car might have wanted. But it doesn't get to choose. It just makes a gasping, choking sound, stops, and won't start up again.

It takes us two hours to push the car along in the road until we find a place that can fix it. I try not to picture myself laughing with Sara and Gus and Macon, our legs dangling in the cool creek. I try not to think of Mr. Shepherd's farm, or fresh strawberries, or cookies.

The man at the gas station has one arm. When he catches me staring at the empty rolled-up sleeve, he says. "The Great War. I'm lucky it was just my arm."

It makes me remember a long time ago when Ma took me to a wax museum in Chicago. There were wax figures of George Washington, Benjamin Franklin, the actress Clara Bow and actor Rudolph Valentino. There were wolf men with hairy faces and vampires with long fangs dripping with blood. And in one whole room were war figures dressed in their uniforms.

The man who ran the museum was also missing an arm, his sleeve folded and neatly pinned. He followed us around in a way that made me know he thought Ma was pretty. In the war room he said, "That war took away my belief in God."

Ma just snorted, like he should be ashamed of himself for saying such a thing. But I could see how he might feel. One archduke over in Europe was assassinated; a world war began. Then millions of men died. I could see how he might lose faith. I've only had a few mishaps and sometimes even *I'm* not sure who God is, *if* He is. It would be nice, once in a while, just to have a little proof.

"The Great War," it is called. It doesn't sound so *great* to me.

Although it's early in the day, it is boiling hot. By now, Macon, Gus, and Sara will have knocked softly on our front door, pressed it open, seen the half-empty room, looked for the space where the car used to be, where grass didn't grow because there was no sun. And Macon will think it's a joke and Gus will cry and Sara will say, "June promised. And now, turns out, she lied."

"Thirty-four dollars," the man says to Pa.

"I'm not asking to build a hotel!" Pa snaps. "Agnes, I told you to save that twenty for a rainy day. . . ."

"It wasn't a rainy day when you were in jail?" she says, and none too kindly. Something is changed in her toward Pa. It's hard to say, exactly. It's like she's not impressed with him anymore. And he senses it. "When she first met me, you'da thought she was meeting Jesus," he once told me. "That's how much she thought of me."

Yes, and I did too. I thought of him as some integral part of God: a finger on God's hand, a toe, even a tongue. But now it's like I'm a scientist and Pa is a set of bones set in front of me to be peered at, examined like a doctor might a patient.

The man just shrugs. "I got to order some parts, and there's labor. . . ."

It is not a permanent death, then. There may still be a resurrection.

The next town is seventeen miles away. The station man says we should stand in the road and look for a ride. We are dirty and worn out. The few cars that pass just whiz right by us like we're invisible.

After a bit, Ma walks onto the road and lies down in the middle of it.

"What on earth are you doing, Agnes?" Pa says.

"I'm tired. That's all. Someone can stop and pick us up or they can run me over."

Rhett tries to give her a hand up but she kicks at him like it's him who made us leave our house.

"Get off the road," Pa says, but he doesn't sound mad, just tired. "I want to tell you about my vision last night.

June, you stand there and wave when a car comes by."

I'd like to kick someone too, but I just walk out in the empty road and look down it. If hell is a flaming pit, and heaven a dazzling cloud, purgatory is a long empty road on a hot day, without a car in sight.

"This is my vision . . . ," Pa says.

It's been a long time since Pa had a vision. When I was little, his visions used to get Ma excited. He'd talk about going someplace where there was a river, or a town square, and of speaking our message to thousands of people. Or he'd envision us in our own white church. It would have a silver steeple and gold sheaves of wheat at the entrance and we'd live in a big clapboard house behind it.

Ma's skin was still pretty then; her eyes would light up and she would say, "Things are going to turn around, Alfred. They sure are." And she would read things in the weather to support her feelings. "The rain is washing away the past," she'd say, or "The sun is shining on our future!"

Now, she just stands up slowly and glares at him. It's like he's trying to sell her an icebox with no door on it and telling her the food's gonna stay cold.

"I saw an amazing place." Pa pauses for effect. "A

paradise with a bright blue sky, white puffy clouds, and a heavenly scent in the air. And that scent was . . . orange blossoms."

"Orange blossoms?"

"And I saw an extraordinary round temple with statues of angels floating all around. Then a real living saint walked out of the temple with her arms wide open to all of us."

"Oh, I get it. I get it now. It's Aimee Semple McPherson you're talking about, isn't it. You'd think she was the Virgin Mary, the way you go on about her."

"All this poverty and she's out in California getting rich!"

"That's because she's famous," Ma hisses. "She's beautiful and she's friends with movie stars."

"And she's feeding people too. While the politicians are telling folks to dig themselves out of their own hole, she's feeding the hungry. She's got folks sleeping in the aisles of her temple. We'll go there! Even if she doesn't hire me right away, we'll have a place to stay."

"She ran off with her lover and pretended it was a kidnapping, and a man died looking for her in the ocean."

"Will you shut up, Agnes."

A cloud of dust moves down the road toward me.

"She's got fat ankles, too," Ma shouts.

A truck appears. Pa pushes me out farther into the road, then Rhett pulls me back. I feel like a rag doll being fought over by two kids.

The truck's brakes screech and the driver swerves. He barely misses me. I think he's going to keep going but then he stops and backs slowly, slowly up. Maybe he feels bad about almost running me over.

The driver waves us to get on the back and we hop on. He *could* be going to California, for all we know, for all he tells us.

Rhett hunkers down in a corner, against a bunch of wire cages with animals in them. I sit by myself in another corner. I don't really want to be near anyone.

The truck pulls back onto the dusty road.

At times like this, tired and downhearted, I wish I had a brother or a sister, someone to take away the boredom from our long travels. Someone little I could take care of. Someone big who could teach me things. I wouldn't even mind being a twin.

Aside from Hari and Kari, I've only met one other set of twins. When we stayed three weeks in Minneapolis once, we lived in the guest house of two old ladies who were twins. They hadn't married, they told me, because they preferred each other's company to anyone else's. They both embroidered and they would switch samplers every hour so that it was never one person's work or the other, but both of theirs.

Of course, Pa and his twin never got along. Pa says it's because his pa loved Abraham better than him. For one thing, there was the mark on Pa's shoulder. For another, Pa stuttered. He had the ideas in his head all right, but when he tried to move them to his tongue, they came out all choppy, "like machine gun fire," he said.

His brother Abraham had a "golden tongue," though. He could talk anyone into anything. He talked the prim girls they met into kisses, their mothers into hot meals and picnics packed to take along the river. He talked his father into loving him most. Maybe if my grandma had lived, Pa could've been *her* favorite, like Jacob was Rebekah's favorite in the Bible. Or maybe she, too, would have been taken in by Abraham's golden tongue.

I was up on the rope when Pa told me all this and I remember saying to him, "Well, Moses stuttered." But Pa just snorted. As much as Pa admires Moses, it's Jesus with whom he compares himself.

And Jesus could talk. Boy could he ever. There's a

reason why everything Jesus said is printed in red in my Bible.

"Sit like a lady, June," Pa calls to me.

I have to stop myself from laughing. I am on the back of a truck on splintery boards with a bunch of pigs, chickens, and roosters. And I should sit like a lady.

I crawl across the truck and look closer into the cages. The pigs look skinny and miserable, but the chickens are fluffy and healthy. As pretty as they are, I'd be happier to see them roasting over a fire. My mouth waters at the thought of it.

There are also two roosters, their feathers rust and copper like blood mixed with gold. Snake Lady said roosters are symbols of an awakening. She had all kinds of ideas about things meaning other things than what they were. Her snakes, she said, were the curving rods of God's tongue.

I do think there's more of God in animals than people. I can see why when Noah got off the ark and let the animals free, he got drunk first chance he could. He must've been heartbroken without them.

The truck jolts to a stop. The driver gestures for us to get out. Before Pa can ask him where we are, he drives off.

Rhett picks up our old battered suitcases, walks down a sloping road, and we follow him. What else can we do?

At the bottom, a little makeshift town appears. Shacks built of all kinds of materials—scrap metal, wood, even fabric—lean up against each other like drunken men. A pile of burnt mattresses is stacked against a dead tree.

Pa creeps up next to me. "You really didn't care all that much for that book, did you?"

A wooden sign with thick black letters welcomes us to our newest destination. And the sign says HOOVERVILLE. Named for the President in these hard times.

Named as a joke.

EVERYONE WHO DRINKS OF THIS WATER
WILL BE THIRSTY AGAIN. . . .

—*BOOK OF JOHN*

President Hoover expects the American people to pull themselves out of poverty by their bootstraps, Ma once said. I try to picture how it would work. You would have to bend over, tug at your own shoes, and try to rise, but it seems physically impossible; you would surely fall. I think of this because, at the entrance of the camp, are a line of worn-out boots. I can't help but imagine that the owners are not among the living.

The place is empty. It is as if the hot sun has dried up all the people like grapes, to raisins, to dust. But that's just how my brain feels in this heat.

We drag our stuff down the long dirt path. Finally, we see a small group sitting around an empty fire pit. The men are all shapes, sizes, and ages. One of them is about as big as a bear. Another is tall and skinny and wears glasses without any lenses. If I were to come up and tap on them, I would poke him in the eye.

The women look like most Midwestern ladies, big and tired and calm, like they've been kneading dough or milking cows.

There is also a little child there, about three, who is covered head to toe in dust. She licks her hand as if it is a lollipop. I heard that some kids are so hungry they are eating their own skin. I hope she doesn't take a bite.

"I come to spread the word of God," Pa says.

"Better to believe in something that doesn't exist than to not believe in something that does," says the man with the glasses.

"Don't mind him," a woman says. "He still thinks he's a professor. Right, Professor?"

"Is there anywhere we can stay for the night?" Pa asks.

"Mr. and Mrs. Chetsky are gone," a white-haired lady suggests. "Their shack is empty, but it needs to be disinfected."

Rhett sets a suitcase down for Ma. She kicks the suitcase, then sits facing away from the people. The suitcase was Pa's wedding present to her all those years ago. Ma told me once how happy it made her when he gave it to her, because she knew that she would travel with him, rather than be left behind like some wives. And when she opened it up, there was the sheet music for all kinds of hymns. She took out the music for "How Great Thou Art" and sang it for him right then and there, and he was so impressed. Of course, the suitcase used to be white and shiny. Now it's practically black from our travels; I don't know what happened to the sheet music.

Ma peers out into the distance as if she expects to see something coming: a train, a man on a horse, a parade.

"You're a preacher?" A lady who looks like a witch points to where some men are digging a hole. "Maybe you could say a word over Mrs. Chetsky."

Pa narrows his eyes. He doesn't like to work for free. Rhett walks over to where the men are digging. He picks up a shovel and helps.

"You'll be wanting some of our grub for your family, I'll bet you a dime . . . ," Witch Lady persists.

"I'll surely oblige." Pa bows.

"The flu," White-Haired Lady explains. "First we had storms so bad you'd expect fish to pour out of the sky. It was like the ocean swept up and poured over our heads. Then the ground dried up like a desert. Next, the flu wasting away the insides of folks. I'm a nurse, and I've never seen the like; it just 'bout cleaned out half the camp, but it's ending now."

"June." Pa starts toward the grave.

"Coming," I call back, but I don't move a muscle.

"Resist." The professor peers at me through his blank glasses. "It's the only way to survive."

"Come on, little girl," White-Haired Lady says to me. "We'll take your stuff to camp. My name's Mrs. Saunders and this here is Mr. Saunders. We've lost our girl."

"Just about your age, she was," Mr. Saunders echoes, his eyes watery.

I look around for Ma, but she has disappeared, leaving her battered suitcase behind. So I follow Mrs. Saunders down the dirt path, where little shacks line up in rows like the boots.

"The Lord is my shepherd . . . ," I hear Pa begin. "I shall not want. . . ."

"Stay away from any camps with a white flag," Mrs. Saunders says. "That means there's sick folks there.

Now, you set your stuff down here, while I go find your mother."

The Chetskys' hut is made of wood and has a shingle roof. It's about as small as an outhouse; maybe two of us could lie down at the same time. If Macon and Gus were here, they could build it into a fort.

Outside is a sorry-looking dogwood tree. I remember they have a lot of those in the South. And at Easter time the white petals bleed at their tips out of sympathy for Christ's torment. Not much good it does Him, though, once he's nailed to a cross, to have petals bleeding on His behalf.

The air inside the shack is as dark as a mine shaft. The whole of life is indecipherable to the human eye, Miss O'Doul said. All we can hope for are minute pieces to fall across our vision, like glass in a kaleidoscope.

Minute. It was a new word for me. It meant tiny, very, very small. Not to be confused with *minute,* the sixty seconds of time ticking off oh so quickly and never to be felt again.

From behind me, I hear a voice, a soft humming of an old hymn. Mrs. Chetsky's lost song fills the air.

19

FOR I HAVE SEEN GOD FACE TO FACE
AND YET MY LIFE IS PRESERVED.

—*GENESIS*

There's a lot of deception in the Old Testament. With his mother's help, Isaac's son Jacob pretends to be his brother Esau in order to cheat him out of his father's blessing.

Later, Jacob falls in love with Rachel and serves her father, Laban, for seven years so he can marry her. But on the wedding night, Laban switches his older daughter Leah in place of Rachel. Jacob wakes up with the wrong bride. He gets to serve yet another seven years for Rachel.

After I am scolded by Ma for entering the Chetskys' hut, Rhett lights a fire and burns the Chetskys' few possessions, then he boils water and cleans the hut.

"I'm beginning to think I was better off in jail," Pa says as he peers inside.

I think about our garden in Michigan, the twin trees, even the outside toilet with the Sears catalogue toilet paper. I think about Gus, Macon, Sara, and Miss O'Doul. That little bit was all I wanted in the world; now it's gone forever. Yeah, he was better off in jail.

"We shouldn't stay here," Ma says. "There's sickness everywhere. Let's walk into town."

"It's twelve miles, and that woman said there'd be a community meal here tonight," Pa says.

"We're going to eat these *sick* people's food? Do you remember Typhoid Mary, the cook who carried the typhoid germ? She kept cooking for families even though it infected them and made them sick or die, until finally she was put in jail."

"What are you talking about, Agnes? We're only here for one night, and I believe it's God's will. You don't think these folks are without assets, do you? Trust me, they're not."

"They're poor as dirt."

"Everyone has something."

"*We* don't."

"June!" Pa digs through the luggage. "We better get to practicing."

There are lots of other deceptions in the Bible.

In Genesis, after their ma is turned into a pillar of salt, Lot's daughters get their pa drunk and sleep with him so they can carry on the family name.

And Tamar, who's lost her husband, tricks her father-in-law, Judah, into sleeping with *her* by pretending to be a prostitute.

Procreating is a real big deal in the Old Testament.

"Where's the rope?" Pa shouts.

Eventually, Jacob gets to have not only Leah and Rachel but also their servants Bilhah and Zilpah, so he comes out all right, like most men. Lot's daughters carry on the family name. Tamar becomes pregnant and once Judah realizes it's his child, he decides not to have her burned to death like he was going to.

"I'm talking to you, June."

But I pretend not to hear. Because while he and Ma were arguing about what to take or not take from the car, I grabbed the rope, opened the trunk of the car, and slipped it right back inside.

Compared to what Jacob did to Esau, Laban to Jacob, and Tamar to Judah, this is nothing.

LIKE A SWALLOW OR A CRANE I CLAMOR,
I MOAN LIKE A DOVE.

—*ISAIAH*

It was Pa's twin Abraham who was supposed to be the preacher. My grandpa believed Abraham's golden tongue and ability to persuade would save souls from hell's fiery flames, plus double the revenues. Pa would be left behind, though; he was supposed to apprentice with a blacksmith in Oklahoma, to sit in front of *real* flames, pound metal, shape nothing into something.

Pa had tried to show my grandpa that he was worthy of following in his footsteps, that it was *him* who was destined to be a preacher. He knew the scripture by heart. He didn't drink or blaspheme. He had nothing to do with women.

The night before he was to be left in Oklahoma, Pa prayed and prayed for God to untangle his tongue, so that maybe he could stay with his pa, bargaining, in that desperate way folks do, that he would devote his life to God.

Miraculously, his prayer was answered. Like the prodigal son in the Bible, Pa's brother Abraham ran away. He met a woman who was in the theater, an actress in fancy clothes. Abraham believed the theater was his calling, not the Word. Later, they found out that he had joined a riverboat show, where he sang and acted in plays and shot a fake gun at the villain. He lived "in sin" with the woman, drank, and smoked. He was sixteen years old.

As soon as it was clear that Abraham was gone for good, Pa opened his mouth and words flowed out like clear water.

My grandpa decided to take Pa along on his travels. But there was one hitch: Grandpa still wouldn't let him preach. He was waiting for Abraham to return. In the meantime, Pa did the same work as Rhett. He put up the tent and passed the collection box. He hung leaflets telling folks where the revivals would be held. He dug waste holes at their camps. He shined his pa's shoes, did the laundry, and cooked.

While Ma rests in the shack and Pa looks for the rope, Rhett and I walk around Hooverville.

Everyone here has a story. There is a man and a woman who lost their farm in Illinois, who have been riding across the country on rickety old bicycles. They have eaten grass and dirt patties seasoned with dandelion greens. They have eaten trash.

There is a fancy lady with high heels. She also took a ride in a truck and was "dumped" here. "Your dad's a looker, even if he don't say much," she whispers to me, as Rhett repairs her roof. I don't bother to correct her.

There's a family here with eight children. The ma's name is Mrs. Fecks. She tells us that they are one of the few families in Hooverville that didn't lose someone to the recent plague. They can all fix watches, Mrs. Fecks tells us, and asks if we have time that needs mending.

Rhett shrugs and takes out his pocket watch. It is silver with his initials carved into it. I have often admired it.

"It was my husband used to make watches. But he ran off from us in Pittsburgh. Can you imagine deserting these children?"

Rhett stares down at his watch like he's seeing it for the first time.

"I don't suppose you've got a match. The light is fading and it's time to light the Sabbath candles."

Rhett searches his pockets and pulls out some matches. He gives them to her.

"Thank you," Mrs. Fecks says.

"Were they Jewish?" I ask Rhett as we walk toward the edge of the camp. He nods.

"How come every religion thinks their way is best?"

He shrugs, then he does it again. He opens his mouth like he's trying to say something.

"What is it, Rhett?"

He points. In the distance, past the end of the camp, is an old car sunk deep into the earth. Its tires are flat, its fender broken, and the side is dented in. It looks like a dead animal that vultures have picked over.

Something about the stripped car seems familiar, and it fills me with sadness, like our travels will not end in the house and church of my imaginings, but here, on a dry earthen plain where even a silver watch with curly initials can't restart the movement of time.

I follow Rhett to the car. He lifts the trunk and pulls out a suitcase and opens it. There are women's clothes, nice ones: a blue and white flowered dress, a yellow blouse, a gray skirt, and a warm wool coat. All of them would be way too big for Ma, though. Just as he reaches for a second suitcase, something rises in the backseat.

Last night I had a dream about the man with the fish hands. I'm stuck in a swamp, looking out a window, when fish skeletons start floating around my head. I swat at them like they're flies, but their numbers increase until they are everywhere. Then he comes, rising from the water like some turkey-necked trout. I think of this dream when I see the white ghostly face with hollow black eyes.

I scream. Rhett drops the suitcase and comes around. He climbs into the car.

When he finally reappears, he is carrying the face, attached to a body, a hollow figure in a wool sweater and trousers.

"Hey, June," Theodore rasps. "Is it already time for our wedding?"

21

O MORTAL, CAN THESE BONES LIVE AGAIN?
—*God speaking to Ezekiel,* EZEKIEL

At the carnival there was a homunculus. It was a painted totem in the shape of a small man. When you opened it, there was a smaller body, then a smaller one. Finally, you'd come upon the real man. He was wrapped tightly like a mummy, only his eyes and mouth showing. I think that's what people are like, and why it's hard to really know them. They have their painted outside, then layers of hidden self.

Life sure can turn on people. The first time I saw Theodore, he looked like a boy in his Sunday best. The car was spanking new. Now he too is stripped down and ravaged. There are no outside layers to protect him.

Theodore wanted to keep his things—his mother's dresses, his clothes, a couple of toys—but Rhett refused. The flu germs could still be alive. Rhett threw everything in a pile and lit fire to it, while Theodore watched and cried.

I understood how he felt. It was the last of his life, his ma. And it makes me think of all the farmers across the country losing their farms, the families losing their homes. I've never had much. Not much to lose, I guess. It's easier that way.

After, Rhett comes back and bends over Theodore. He feels his head and frowns. Theodore reaches up and puts his arm around Rhett, so I guess he doesn't hold it against him, that Rhett burned his things. Rhett hugs him back, then he motions for me to mind Theodore, but not get too close to him.

"I'm sorry about your ma." I sit down beside him, anyway.

"You know what I've figured out?" he whispers.

"What?"

"You can't count on anything. The day before my dad died, I heard him tell my mom that sixty men were laid off at the mine. He had fired them himself, writing a message on a slip of paper and handing it to them as they left for the day. He said that since he was foreman, he would never be laid off and she could go out and buy a new dress to celebrate. She was pretty happy about that. But the next day, it must've been the ones who was laid off that was happy, because the mine caved in and everyone down there was killed."

"Yeah, you never know."

"What do you think happens after you die?" he says.

"Pa says that if you're good, you float into the air and feathery creatures meet you and carry you to heaven. But if you're bad you plummet into a smoldering pit and burn in agony until the end of time, which is forever."

"That seems like a pretty big punishment, don't you think?"

"Yeah, but think about the punishment for just one bite of an apple—then it makes a bit more sense."

"I might die."

"Maybe," I agree.

"But if I don't, it was you and Rhett saved me. I'll always remember that. And now I know he's gonna look after me. I know it even though he didn't say so."

"Rhett doesn't talk," I explain.

"Did someone cut out his tongue?"

"No. He can talk. He just doesn't. I don't know why."

"Maybe he's afraid of what he'll say."

22

I AM POURED OUT LIKE WATER. . . .

—*PSALM 22*

I've never understood Jesus' parable of the prodigal son. The one son is good and stays and serves his father. The other son is sinful; he squanders his property on prostitutes and runs off. When the sinful son returns, though, the father throws a big party and celebrates. He forgives him everything.

It's like how some folks believe that you can be a horrible person your whole life, then if you ask for forgiveness at the last minute, you get into heaven same as anyone else, same as the person who has given to the poor, been kind to the sick and the old, taken care of their family. It just doesn't seem fair.

Maybe God just likes a chance to show how nice He can be.

Pa's twin, Abraham, was kind of like the prodigal son, but he never got the fun of having a party.

After Abraham ran off, four years passed. Then, one day, when Pa and my grandpa were in Mississippi on their travels, they heard about the showboat. Two men said that there was someone acting in plays on it that looked just like Pa.

My grandpa figured it had to be Abraham. So he and Pa camped out at the dock to wait for the riverboat's return. My grandpa told Pa, "When he gets back, it'll be time for you to move on. I can only carry one of you, and it's going to be him."

"What if he won't come?" Pa asked. In answer, my grandpa pulled out a pistol. Abraham wouldn't have a choice.

All night they sat up and watched for the showboat. The weather was warm. Mosquitoes landed on their arms, their necks. There were so many of the insects, they gave up slapping at them and just let them feast on their blood.

In the morning, when the boat still hadn't returned, my grandpa went into town to get supplies.

Pa sat by the river, washing clothes. The air was the color of metal. Black clouds moved like funeral cloth across the sky. Just as Pa pulled the last shirt from the river, he saw something floating in the water.

At first, Pa thought it was a misshapen log. Then he noticed the suit clothes flapping on the surface, like so many flags waving in the water. The corpse was facedown, the hands and the body bloated, balloon-like.

Normally, Pa would have just let it be. *Let the dead bury the dead,* he might have thought. But something prompted him. I guess those were the days when he still had feelings like I have, that guided his actions like a cane tapping out a blind man's path.

Pa waded in. He grabbed hold of the stiff arms. It took him a few tries to pull the waterlogged corpse from the river.

The face of the man was blue and swollen with fluid and death and cold. Part of the skin was eaten away. Even so, Pa knew immediately who it was. It was easy to recognize his own face.

He dragged the corpse onto the bank.

The body of one brother had found its way to another, like they were still tied together by an invisible cord. But Pa didn't think about that. It was only later that he would tell me that Abraham came to him because "blood is thicker than water. You can't escape it."

But at the time, all Pa could think about was trouble. He knew that he was in it, even though he had done nothing to bring about this disaster.

He was right. When my grandpa came back and saw the double image of his sons, one dead and one alive, he grabbed the nearest tree branch and beat Pa until he was bloody.

I remember asking Pa then why his father would respond this way. "Simple," Pa said, like he was telling me a recipe for apple pie. "He figured the wrong son had died."

Rhett builds a lean-to against the dogwood tree, to keep him and Theodore dry. Every day I ask Rhett if Theodore is going to die and every day he shakes his head to say he doesn't know. Today, when I come and visit, I ask the same question. But this time, Rhett just smiles.

There's color back in Theodore's face. He is allowed to stand up and walk the few feet to our shed, but Ma won't let him inside. She's worried about germs.

"Where's Pa?" I ask. For some reason, Theodore gets under his skin. He's already told Rhett that we're not dragging along another mouth to feed, let alone a sick one.

"Mr. Saunders rode off this morning to see if the car is fixed," Ma says. "It's been hours and he's still not back, so Alfred went to look for him. I'm going inside to lie down. This heat . . ." Ma gets up slowly and moves inside.

"What do you want to be when you grow up?" Theodore says.

"My friends in Michigan used to ask each other that."

"I'm fourteen. It's all I think about."

"Do you get to *choose*?"

"Sure. Why not?"

"I thought your parents choose for you." After I say that I feel bad, because he doesn't have parents anymore.

"Nah," he says. "But maybe it's different for girls. Maybe girls don't get to choose."

"Yeah." I try to think of girls I know of who got to choose. There aren't very many. Snake Lady seemed to do what she wanted, but her husband was dead. I guess Aimee Semple McPherson does what she wants, although it was her ma who wanted her to preach. In the Bible, there's only Deborah I can think of, the prophetess and judge. She sits under a palm tree telling people what to do. When she wants to start a war, she just calls up a man and says it's time. He insists she come along and they win the war.

"I think I'll be president and you can be first lady," Theodore says. "But I won't be like Hoover. I'll be like Abraham Lincoln. Only nobody is going to shoot me while I'm watching a play, because I'm not going to go to the theater. Ever."

"Yeah."

"For a while, I didn't think I was going to get to grow up."

"Where's Agnes?" Pa comes up. He's carrying a paper sack.

"Lying down."

"You know how much that robber wants to fix that car?" he says. "Thirty dollars."

"That's less than he said," I offer.

"We're gonna head to California no matter how we get there." Pa sets the bag down. "And look, June: Mr. Saunders brought back your rope."

The rope spills out of the bag like a snake.

The air is so hot and heavy; it is like we are

swimming underwater. There are times when I'm in a place and it will light right up like someone has poured gold over it. A river, a pasture, trees, become absolutely clear to me, and I am sure it is God's light, God's presence.

This isn't one of those times.

23

MY HEART IS LIKE WAX
IT IS MELTED WITHIN MY BREAST.

—*PSALM 22*

The New Testament is so much shorter than the Old. I guess there's just one story told there, pretty much. What I wonder about, though, is what's left out, like what did Jesus do the first thirty or so years of his life? Did he go to school? Have friends? Was he married? Did he have children? Jesus asks his followers to shed their lives. Did he do the same?

Pa decides to wait until after the relief truck comes to hold a revival. When people have full stomachs, they are more likely to share what little they might be hoarding.

Theodore and I sit side by side drinking milk and

eating biscuits and watery mashed potatoes. Old Mr. Turner walks by. He used to have a parrot that sat on his shoulder, Mrs. Saunders told me, and he still talks to it like it's there. "Give 'em hell, Sparky," he instructs the parrot. "Goddamn right."

"Boy, my dad would'a washed my mouth out with soap if I said the G word combined with damn," Theodore says.

"Mine too."

"But what I think is really bad is when people use God's name to be bad, and to do wrong things."

"Like what?"

"Like wars . . . or like making people do things they don't want to." He picks up a stick and draws circles in the dirt.

"Why are you drawing all those circles?"

"Things going round, coming back. You ever hear of reincarnation?"

"What's that?"

"It's where you die and your soul returns to life as something else, like a baby, or a dog, or a rock."

"There might be some advantage to being a rock."

As if to show me how wrong I am, Theodore picks up a rock and throws it. "Rhett's gonna take me to my aunt in Seattle."

My tongue is a rock.

"We're hitching a ride with someone who's going to Colorado tomorrow. It's gonna be hard to leave you, June."

"How do you know he's taking you?" I finally say.

"He said so. He said, 'I'll take you to find your aunt.' You know your dad won't let me come along with you."

"Rhett doesn't speak."

"He spoke to me. His voice came out kind of rusty, but he spoke."

"He couldn't have."

"He did. Come with us, June," he urges. "Your dad don't care nothing about you 'sides what he can use you for."

"That's not true!" Before I know what is happening, I reach out and shove him. He lands on the ground.

"I'm sorry, June."

"My folks need me."

"I know."

I give him a hand up. "He's my pa."

"I know."

"It's so hot," I say. "It's hard to think."

Theodore brushes himself off. "Remember, June, I'm gonna marry you someday."

"But how will we find each other?"

"Same way as before," he says. "God will help us."

"You don't believe in God."

"I decided I *would* believe in God. I decided it's easier that way."

"Can you do that? Just change your mind?"

"Sure, but just in case, let's set a date. Meet me back at this Hooverville."

"When?"

"April tenth, my birthday, 1937. By then, we'll be old enough—no one can tell us what to do."

Rhett comes up then. He has his satchel on his back and one of the suitcases. "Rhett," I say, the rock in my mouth melting, turning to water in my eyes.

He puts his hands on my shoulders and I know that he wants what Theodore wants, that I go with them.

"But Seattle is so far." I sob into his chest. "It will take too long for you to come back."

"We'd better go, Dad." Theodore says. *Dad?* I step back.

Dad.

"I sure wish I had a picture of you, June," Theodore says. "Do you have a photograph?"

I shake my head. At the carnival there was a man

who had a big camera on three legs that made a great *poof* of smoke. Eventually, an image would appear on paper like some kind of miracle.

But God doesn't approve of graven images, Pa said, so I've never had a photograph taken. *Graven*—as in engraved, I guess. Not *grave*—the hole in which the dead are buried. Nor *gravity*—which can mean seriousness of mind, or the force that pulls me, that pulls all of us, to the earth.

24

DO NOT LISTEN TO THE WORDS OF THE
PROPHETS WHO PROPHECY
TO YOU! THEY ARE DELUDING YOU. . . .
—*JEREMIAH*

Of all the books in the Bible, the Book of Ruth is my favorite. When her husband dies, Ruth insists on following her mother-in-law, Naomi, to Israel. Naomi tells Ruth that she's free and she should find her own fortune, but Ruth remains loyal, saying, "Where thou goest, I will go. . . ." Ruth then goes to the field of Naomi's relative, Boaz, and collects sheaves of wheat to feed her and Naomi. At night, she climbs into bed with him. Boaz marries her and Ruth and Naomi are cared for.

Pa followed *his* father loyally around the country as he preached, just like we follow Pa now. After Abraham's death, his pa grew even more fervent in his belief, more stringent in his schedule, moving from place to place daily, sometimes without food or sleep, preaching God's word.

It was good training for him, Pa told me.

Usually, Pa had to stay out of sight at the revivals, but once in a while, my grandpa would let him come forward and say a few words of introduction.

Pa always says he was born to preach, that it's in his blood, but one time he admitted that it was something he had to earn.

At this very moment he is mumbling and pacing back and forth under the dogwood tree. Ma is sitting on the ground in front of him, an audience of one.

"In the whole land, says the Lord, two thirds shall be cut off and perish and one third shall be left alive," Pa recites from Zechariah. "And I will put this third into the fire, refine them as one refines silver, and test them as gold is tested."

"Which third are we?" Ma asks, her voice dry as the ground.

I've never seen Pa's hands shake before, but this time, as he picks up the rope, it moves in little jumps like a snake prodded with a wire.

There was a man at one of the soup kitchens

whose hands shook like that. He said it was because liquor had poisoned his system.

But Pa doesn't drink. "I'll hang the rope by the fire pit," Pa says. "There are two sturdy trees there, though they're about dead. Darn that Rhett, always disappearing just when we need him."

"When don't we?" Ma says.

It has been three days since Rhett and Theodore left, and all three days the sky poured down tears. Everyone in the camp stood out in that rain, being washed, drinking it. Now the sun is so scorching that the earth is hard again. It's as if it never rained at all.

Pa stumbles down the path. Yesterday, I heard Witch Lady refer to him as "that old preacher bum."

"I'm just going to close my eyes a minute," Ma says.

I sit next to her so she can rest her head on my lap. "Ma?" I stroke her hair.

"What?"

"Have you ever heard Rhett speak?"

"'Course I have. He spoke all the were young. Full of ideas, he was."

What is Rhett's voice like? I voice? Macon said it comes Pa thinks it comes from G

sound is waves moving through the air, just like water washes up onto the shore, then slides back into the sea.

"He spoke to Theodore," I say, but Ma doesn't answer. I shake her shoulder.

"Did he?" she says.

"Yes."

"He was quite taken by the boy, wasn't he?" She opens her eyes.

"How does Rhett find us?"

"I write to him. That's how. Or I phone, if I can manage it, or send a telegram. And if you ever tell your pa, I'll break both your arms."

"Break my *legs,* then I won't have to perform."

"Very funny, June. Your performance is the only way we'll get water from these rocks. Besides, it's what makes you special."

"Do you think anyone here has *money*?"

"You'd be surprised, June. Why, just yesterday, your pa saw Mr. Saunders sell some medicine to Mr. Turner for a dollar!"

"Where do you write to Rhett?"

"At his mother's. Even if he's not there, he calls her finds out our plan. She gives him money, too. Not because she wants him to come home for good.

Her husband was in manufacturing before he died. She's got a store in Providence."

"But why does Rhett follow us the way he does, if he could be living in Providence?"

"Because he decided to serve your pa's mission. Because he wants to make amends."

"For what?"

Ma shrugs.

"I don't understand. . . ."

"What makes you think you have to understand things, June? Don't you think you might just be better off not knowing about things all the time?"

"No."

"You're tiring me," Ma says. It's something she says often, but looking at her, I know it is true. She has grown thinner, if it's possible. She coughs loudly. "Fetch me a rag, June. I don't know what all is coming out of my chest."

This time, I keep quiet while she sleeps. The sky lowers over us like a gray cloth. Pa appears in front of me.

"It's time, June. If we wait much longer, it'll be pitch dark. We gotta move them tonight or they're not like to share anything. We gotta get our car back. Where's your costume?"

"It doesn't fit anymore."

"What did Ma feed you while I was away? Steak and ice cream?" Pa puts his hand on top of my head as if to stop me from growing.

"Ma's asleep."

Pa peers down at her. "She had the prettiest face when I met her, a face like yours, and a voice to match. Sometimes, it's hard to keep faith."

FOLLOW ME AND I WILL MAKE YOU FISH FOR PEOPLE.
—*Jesus speaking to Simon and Andrew,* MARK

In fairy tales, sometimes, people have to give up their babies. They have made a bad deal with an enchantress or a goblin. Their newborn daughter is sent to a tower to do nothing but grow her hair or to the woods, where her hands are cut off, her mouth sewn shut.

Still, I wish someone would give me up. I would take my chances.

Or Jesus might say, *Follow me,* and I would do it, just for a change.

From up in this tree, I look down upon the shaky structures of the camp. I try to think of what lies beyond, but the world seems to end right here and now, like when a thread disappears on a cloth and you can't see where it starts up again.

Sitting on the ground by the fire pit, waiting, is the population of Hooverville: men, women, children, a stray dog that looks like a starved deer. This *is* a large audience. They have nothing else to do.

Pa starts slowly; he always does. His eyes lowered, his voice soft, he recites from Mark: "Those who are well have no need for a physician. . . ."

I used to be more comfortable on the tightrope than anywhere else. But now, out of practice, my body taller, heavier, the rope feels like a distant relative who may not be as nice as I remembered. Like I might meet up with Big Ben and he'd cuss like a prison guard. Or Snake Lady. And she'd put one of her snakes on me.

"You've heard that angels fly." Pa gestures toward heaven. "Now my June will show you the lightness of the spirit, the ease of God's grace."

My foot touches the rope.

Like Theodore says, you never know how things are gonna work out. Joseph could've died in the prison before anyone found out he could interpret dreams. Abraham might have slaughtered Isaac before God got a chance to stop him. There *could* have been heads in Mr. Shepherd's cellar. The disciples might have told

Jesus no, they would rather stay put with their families than follow him around, and not know where they'd sleep or when they'd eat, and be spit on, and wear out their sandals.

"Submit your will to God," Pa says.

But what does that really mean? Is it God's will for these people to give us their money, so we can get our car and leave?

Heat rises toward me. Summer calls to fall. Leaves dry on their branches so slowly we can't see, but only hear them in our sleep, the tiny cracking apart, like a door opening that in a dream becomes a mouse, a rooster, a window out of which you are climbing, sliding down a tree, tumbling in your dreams toward other dreams, looking for your own shadow in the evening light. And not seeing it anywhere.

"But man is depraved," Pa shouts. "Sin brings hell unto earth in fire and strife and hunger! Who among us has not sinned?"

I have never looked down before. It was something Pa taught me: Never look down. If you do, you will see the eyes of strangers, lose balance, lose grace.

But these are not strangers, these people with whom I've lived for two weeks. So I look, and there they are: Mrs. and Mr. Saunders, Mrs. Fecks and her children, Witch Lady, Mr. Turner, and the professor peering up at me with his hands shaped like binoculars.

Holding life together. That is what they are all doing in their own way. And that is what I am doing.

But how nice it would feel to let go, to not worry about Ma or have to please Pa.

It is almost dark. Beneath my feet, the rope is barely visible. The heat from the earth rises toward the end of summer. The earth below me like a ball of blue coral.

"She's going to fall," Mrs. Saunders cries out.

Their faces rise to meet me.

THEIR VOICE HAS GONE OUT TO ALL THE EARTH
AND THEIR WORDS TO THE ENDS OF THE WORLD.

—*ROMANS*

"Where have you been?" Macon says.

"We've been looking for you," Gus adds.

Fish Man flaps his fins in applause.

"Make him go away," I beg Gus.

"Why didn't you come with us?" Theodore appears.

"I wanted to."

"Then come. You still can."

I try to get up but Macon, Sara, and Gus surround me. "Stay with us."

"What do you want, sugar?" a voice says.

"We've been worried about you," Hari and Kari say as they arrive.

"You haven't been eating enough greens," Hari says.

"Your blood is too thin," Kari adds.

"You wear your feelings on the outside of your skin."

"I'm scared," I admit.

"Give her some scripture, Kari. That'll make her feel better."

"The descendents of Shem: Elam, Asshur, Lud, and Aram."

"Not the begets, you idiot!"

"Rhett . . ."

"Make her open her eyes," Mrs. Saunders says. "If we let her sleep, she may not wake up again."

"Wake her!" Ma shouts.

"Open your eyes, June," Fish Man says.

"I don't want to."

"Get the medicine, Frank."

"Sit up."

"Feel this bump on her head."

"Open your eyes."

The first face I see is Ma's.

"Sit up, honey," Mrs. Saunders says.

"Let her sleep." Pa's voice is strained, as if at any moment the strings will snap.

"Two heads are better than one," Hari and Kari say, then they disappear into the dark air.

"I've got something that will shore her up," Mr. Saunders says.

"Theodore?"

"Drink this soup." Ma lifts the cup to my mouth. The hot liquid slides down my throat.

"Rhett . . ."

"He's not here."

"I saw him."

"Scare me to death . . . ," Ma says.

"Do I have the flu?"

"You fell."

I look around the room. Next to where I lie there's bread, fruit, one of Mrs. Saunders's bottles of medicine.

Pa is in the corner, examining the rope. "There's something wrong with it," he says. "There has to be."

"My head hurts."

"It's a concussion."

"She's fine," Pa says. "Aren't you, June? You'll be back on the rope in no time."

"No, Pa. I won't."

"'Course you will. If you fall off a horse—"

"This is not the time," Mrs. Saunders admonishes him.

"I'm just done with it," I say, feeling like Hansel and Gretel shoving the witch into her own oven.

"Now, come on," says Mrs. Saunders, leading Pa and Mr. Saunders out of our shack with an authority that surprises me. "You menfolk can just wait outside."

To my surprise, Pa leaves. But I can still see the shadow of him pacing outside the small window.

"Of all the things." Witch Lady shakes her head.

Mrs. Saunders brings more of the hot soup to my mouth. "Drink, honey."

"What else hurts?" Ma asks, her eyes dark, her face flushed, her whole body shivering beneath her shawl.

"Nothing. I'm okay."

"Get up now, then, if you're better," Ma says weakly. "I need to take your place."

Mrs. Saunders looks at Ma like she's seeing her for the first time. She puts her hand on Ma's forehead.

"Lord Almighty," she cries. "She's on fire!"

27

FORGIVE US OUR TRESPASSES.

—*LUKE*

Belief is a word I have a lot of trouble with. How can you believe something just because you're told? *Faith* is a little bit easier. Like I may not *believe* it when Pa says he has a vision and our life is going to get better. But I might have faith that *something* will work out, that life is not just going to end here.

Once, I heard voices singing in a church, but when I went inside it was empty. Another time, when I was feeling low, a gold leaf floated onto my lap, even though there wasn't a tree around for miles.

Stones, leaves, songs, something wraps round me, like an invisible coat. And I might call that God. Or my head suddenly clears of its wild racing thoughts and an answer comes to me. I might call that God too. And that is the best I can do.

There is now a white flag outside our shack. Only Mrs. Saunders comes to join us. She brings soups and medicines, while Pa goes on and on about better times. "Remember that time I was preaching in Minneapolis?" Pa says to Ma. "The rain was so bad that they let me preach in the hall. The sign was up that said 'Potluck Supper.' The date had melted, so folks thought it was that night, and they poured in with their plates of grub and people ate supper. I preached while they were eating, plates and forks banging away, but after a while you could've heard a pin drop."

Ma coughs.

"Put out that cigarette," Mrs. Saunders commands Pa. "There's little enough air in here as it is."

She's the only person I've ever seen boss Pa. Pa tosses his cigarette outside. I remember that Ma used to light his cigarettes. She would take one out and put it in her mouth and light it, then give it to him. He thought it was funny, to see a cigarette in her mouth.

"This isn't the flu," Mrs. Saunders says. "These aren't the symptoms."

Pa peers at Mrs. Saunders with the stunned expression that is frozen on his face lately. It's like he thinks that if he moves, his skin will crack. "Then, what is it?"

"If it's tuberculosis, there's a charitable hospital in town that will take her in."

"It's not tuberculosis." Pa swats his hand in the air, as if Mrs. Saunders is a fly and she should shoo.

"Wouldn't it be good if Ma could go to the hospital?" I ask Pa after Mrs. Saunders leaves.

"It's run by those folks who bring the food out here, the Catholics," he says with disgust. "A convent."

"What's wrong with Catholics?"

"They categorize sin, have three columns for it. They love Mary more than Jesus."

"What difference does it make, if Ma gets better?"

"They still pack 'em in at the churches. Give folks a warm room, a few candles. In Houston once, I preached to a crowd of forty."

"What does that have to do with Ma?"

"I'm going outside to smoke," he says. "She'll be all right."

She won't, I want to scream. *She'll be like Mrs. Chetsky and Theodore's ma. Rhett would take her to the hospital!*

All day I sit in the shed next to Ma and recite the Book of Ruth to her. Ruth is the noblest character in the Old Testament because she puts her devotion to her mother-in-law above herself.

I don't remember falling asleep, but when I wake up, it's dark. Pa's bed is empty and Ma is completely still.

"Ma!" I light a candle.

"He leaves every night," Ma whispers. "Just gets up and walks out the door and doesn't come back until dawn."

"Pa?"

"You know how he doesn't like to stay put. It's his restlessness. He thinks God is something to be chased down, like a sheriff tracks a criminal."

"I love you, Ma."

"I know that, June. And don't think it hasn't given me pleasure. When I was a little girl, I thought about heaven all the time. I loved going to church, singing the hymns, feeling the spirit. I guess it's easier to feel the spirit on a full stomach."

"Guess so," I admit.

"Having you was the closest to heaven I ever got. Especially when you were all mine, before your pa got so interested in having you in the show. But what's sad is that here I am dying, and I'm gonna go to the other place. That's what's so sad. Blessed are those who die when they're children, before they have a chance to sin."

"Ma, you don't mean hell?"

"Where else would I go? I'm going to be punished for my sins. Or," she admits, "maybe if I'm lucky I'll end up someplace in between. So, this is my advice to you: Be good."

"I don't believe that God is like that, that He punishes people for nothing. I don't even believe in hell. It's just something made up to make people behave."

"June, how can you blaspheme this way?"

"I'm not blaspheming. What's the point of faith and good behavior if it's just to earn some final prize. If you behave right it should be for the love of God and for justice, not just to get into heaven."

Rather than get mad, Ma smiles. "I guess maybe you'll be a preacher after all."

"No. I won't. I want to be at teacher like Miss O'Doul."

She grabs my hand. "I will tell you, June, I'd do it all again. I'd do it again, because if I didn't there wouldn't be *you*!"

"What do you mean?"

"And when I'm gone, I want you to remember me kindly." Ma coughs. Blood speckles the blanket.

"Ma!"

"Isn't it funny? First you lying here and me thinking you were gonna die. Now me, really dying."

"Don't say that. You can't. You can't leave me with . . ."

"With *him*? I know. And I'm sorry that I didn't stick up for you more. He came to me when I was weak and low, and I thought God had sent him, but maybe . . ." She looks around the room. Her voice gets so soft I have to lean into her face to hear her. "Listen," she whispers, "this is what I want to tell you. It's important. Not even your pa knows this. . . ."

"What?"

"And I never want him to, because, well, he hasn't had much in this life and you know that. You and me. We're all he has."

"What is it?"

"You were with me already. When I met him."

"What do you mean?"

"You were *with* me. It couldn't have been but two or three weeks, but I could feel you, a little whirlwind in my stomach. Retching first thing in the morning.

Dizzy all afternoon. And I knew you were a girl. I *knew* it."

"You mean Pa—"

"I was on my own," she interrupts. "You understand. One man had failed me, but in your pa, I thought I was being saved by *God*."

"You mean you were *pregnant* before you got married?"

"June, don't use such an impolite word. I raised you better than that."

"But what are you saying?"

"What I'm saying, June, is you don't have to become a preacher. It's not in your blood. He's not really your pa."

"He's not my pa?"

"He's thinks you're his, and he's taken care of you like a pa, so in some ways he is." She lets go of my hand. "Just not in a blood way."

"But . . ."

She closes her eyes. Her chest makes a sound like an accordion having the air pressed out of it, without a note being played.

"Ma," I hiss. "You can't die."

But she doesn't answer me.

She doesn't answer me, but the answer does come,

in the voice, the surprising little voice that drops into my head as easily as a gold leaf dropping onto my lap from nowhere. And I know it then. She's not going to die.

And now I know something else.

28

I WILL HAVE MERCY ON WHOM I HAVE MERCY
AND I WILL HAVE COMPASSION ON WHOM
I HAVE COMPASSION.

—*ROMANS*

I've been thinking about angels. It's the only way I can imagine that God has time to guide all these people, let alone animals, insects, and anything else that might strike His fancy.

Maybe angels are good people who have died. Or maybe they're separate creations. Maybe angels get inside living people and make them do good things, like the devil might take someone over so they will sin.

Like Rhett is being an angel to Theodore. And Mrs. Saunders to us.

Three days after Mrs. Saunders talks about the

hospital, a white van comes. There is a cross on the side of it.

Pa doesn't thank Mrs. Saunders or even say good-bye. He just stares at the ground and smokes while two men carry Ma right on her cot into the van. Pa and I gather our things, then I kiss Mrs. Saunders good-bye, but like Rhett, I don't speak. How can you thank an angel? I climb into the van next to Ma. Then Pa climbs in. We are finally leaving Hooverville.

The convent is down a long dirt road lined with trees. It makes me happy to see Ma watching the trees through the window. As soon as the van pulls up to the convent, a nun comes out. Ma is admitted to the hospital right away. The nun instructs Pa on how to get to town. Aside from the doctor and priests, men are not allowed inside the convent. Even the men who drove the van have to wait outside, while a group of nuns carries Ma into the building.

"Let's go, June," Pa says.

"Where?"

Pa jangles the last couple of coins from the night I fell.

"Autumn will be setting upon us in no time," he says, and starts down the dirt road.

I stand for a moment, then follow him.

The whole time we're walking, Pa goes on and on about how inconvenient it is of Ma to get sick just when our luck is turning around and we're heading West. I wonder what luck he might be talking about. The phrase *heading West* reminds me of Pa's story.

After Pa's brother Abraham died, he and my grandpa moved farther south. For a long time, my grandpa complained of the cold. It could be a hundred degrees outside, sweat pouring off their skin in buckets, and he would be shivering. Pa believed that the icy water of the Mississippi River was flowing through his pa's veins.

They moved through the Carolinas, Georgia, and Louisiana. In Florida, they preached in the swamps, where alligators silently floated, their jaws opening and closing like guillotines. One morning, Pa woke up to find that his tent had sunk into the soft earth. Only a few yards away, a hotel was being constructed. And there he was, sinking.

The air was so moist that morning that for a second he thought he was in the water, that he was drowning like his brother—he didn't know how to swim.

Finally, he came to his senses and climbed out. A

note was stuck to the tent. It was from his pa. It said, *Too cold here. Heading West. Catch up with me sometime.*

Pa had lived every moment of his life with his father. He had imitated his preaching, accepted his beliefs, and been loyal to his mission. But after that day, he never saw him again, only read the account of his death in Utah in a circular on evangelism.

"Wait here," Pa tells me.

"Huh?"

I realize that the whole time I've been walking, I have been looking at my feet, lost in thought. I haven't heard a word he's said.

Pa disappears into a small diner. There is a big red sign in front of it. A fish wears a hat and carries a fishing pole as if he is going to catch food rather than be eaten. The sign says FRIED FISH AND HASH BROWNS. NOTHIN' LIKE IT. It reminds me of the passage in Mark, when Jesus comes upon Simon and Andrew. The two brothers are fishing and Jesus says to them, "Follow me and I will make you fish for people."

When I first heard that, I was pretty confused. I thought that Jesus was telling them to become food on someone's plate. I was young. Pa was more patient back then. When I asked him why they should be turned into food, he just laughed and laughed. It was the last time I remember him laughing.

Pa comes back. "I've got a ride for us as far as Texas. We just got to wait for the driver to finish his lunch. From Texas, it should be easy to find a truck to California. If need be, we can ride the rails."

"We're leaving *now*?"

"That's what I've been saying the last twenty minutes."

"But—"

"There's nobody hungry in California. You can just walk up to a tree and pick fruit."

"But what about Ma?"

"When she's better, we'll send for her. It's not like we're abandoning her. We'll find a place and set things up nicely for her, then she'll come."

"But the car—"

"We'll never earn enough here to get the car back. Look at this place. This city's one giant funeral, what with that flu that swept through. And if we get stuck here this winter—"

"But Rhett will come back here to find us."

"I don't give a hoot what Rhett does. I'm tired of his running off every chance he gets."

He doesn't know, Ma said. *He still thinks he's my pa.*

What if I tell him right now? *I don't belong to you. I never have. You don't get to tell me what to do.*

"I don't want to go."

"Look, I know you don't want to walk the tightrope. You're a young lady now. I understand. I'll throw it away. We'll burn it. I have new ideas. It'll be *you* who does the preaching. You've got it already. The spirit. The scripture. We'll go to Aimee Semple McPherson. She'll be your guide. She won't be able to resist. You'll have beautiful clothes and we'll eat in fine restaurants. . . ."

When Aimee Semple McPherson escaped her kidnappers, she walked through the desert in Mexico and appeared in a village, her clothes unrumpled, her shoes perfectly white. Was that a miracle, like she said, or was it a hoax, like the press accused?

"I'm staying here with Ma. Like when you were in jail and we stayed near you!"

Pa lifts his hand. I can feel the *whoosh* of air that comes before a slap, feel the pain before it reaches me, but it doesn't come.

"June. Please." He lowers his hand. "I can barely even breathe without Agnes. My voice is going out on me. I'm fifty years old. That jail broke me 'bout in two. Who is going to listen to the spirit in *me*?"

"Pa, don't cry. Please—"

"I've been places where fish disappeared from the stream. People were greedy. They took nets and ravished the stream. That's how I feel about God. There's too many of us calling on Him, too much misery. Not enough to go around. But you're young. You can still call and He'll listen. . . ." His voice breaks into sobs. "God loves youth, June, like everyone else—youth and beauty."

"I don't know what you're talking about."

The driver of the truck comes out of the diner and signals to us.

"Please, June! I know you don't have to come. The whole world is at your disposal."

The driver honks the horn.

"Pleease," he begs.

"Okay, Pa. Fine. Let's go. The man's ready."

Pa stumbles toward the truck.

How can I leave him alone?

29

VERY TRULY, I TELL YOU, ONE OF YOU WILL BETRAY ME.

—*Jesus speaking to his disciples*, BOOK OF MATTHEW

There are a lot of other deceptions in the Bible. Like when Abraham is traveling with his wife in Egypt. His wife is beautiful and he's afraid men's jealousy will provoke them to do him harm, so he pretends that she's his sister. The Pharaoh takes her then, and sleeps with her, bringing God's wrath on him and his people for this adultery. Finally, Abraham admits Sarah is his wife. The Pharaoh is angry, but lets them leave in peace. The Bible never says what Sarah thinks about all this.

Or like when King David falls in love with Bathsheba. In order to get rid of Bathsheba's husband,

Uriah, King David has him sent to the battlefield to be killed. In the process, other innocent soldiers die.

The Old Testament is full of stuff like that.

And then there's the biggest deception in the New Testament: Judas betraying Jesus.

The truck on which we're riding seems to make its way through every street and alley. It's like the driver is taking himself on a sight-seeing tour. There is no door to the back, so if he makes a sudden stop, we could roll out. Although the truck smells like apples, there is no cargo, except for a small shrine in the corner, where there is a little table stuck to the floor, with candles and a statue of the Virgin Mary glued onto it, her arms outstretched, like an opera star singing to a crowd.

There are three Marys in the New Testament: the Virgin Mary, Mary Magdalene, and a third one known as the "other Mary."

Everyone knows about Mother Mary, and how she became pregnant by the Holy Ghost, even though she wasn't married. I've often wondered what the other people in her town thought about that. Did they believe she was still a virgin, like Joseph did? The angel couldn't have come to explain it to *all* of them. I wonder if they were mean to her. Whatever the case, she must've been scared. Like Ma was when she was pregnant with me.

Half of this city is boarded up. The other half is bustling with people. The air smells like fish, old clothes, and spices. Sara's ma made the best spice cookies. And Sara used to share them with me from her lunch pail. And Macon's ma made cucumber sandwiches. In Michigan, Rhett cooked a turkey that was so tender it tasted like butter.

My stomach feels carved out. I don't remember when I last ate.

The driver stops frequently. He doesn't check with us or explain. We might as well be a couple of sheep.

Pa sits at the very back of the truck bed. His mouth is open. He is mumbling softly. The only word I can make out is *Agnes*. It takes me a second to figure out that he's asleep. I think about his wandering, nights when Ma was lying in the hut, his inability to rest. He does love her. He loves us both, after all, in his own way.

The air is hot and so dry; my tongue feels like a wad of cotton. The metal floor of the truck bed is sizzling. Mrs. Saunders said we would have an Indian summer. She could tell by the way the moon seemed to float in the sky and by the parched summer air, the way even the mosquitoes would dry up like specks of dust. When she said that, I pictured a bunch of men on horses riding through the Hooverville dirt with big feathered headdresses. Still, an Indian summer would postpone the cold weather that Pa is so afraid of.

The driver pulls over and runs into a house. I crawl over to Mary and try to make out her face in the darkness. Gus told me that there's a statue of Mary someplace in France that actually talks. And there are girls in the world who bleed from the palms of their hands in sympathy with Christ.

Each snore coming out of Pa's mouth sounds different than the one before. One is a baby rattle, the next an engine starting, the next a bear groaning. He can't even sleep with any certainty. It makes me feel sad for him—the unevenness of his life, how people stopped listening to his words of God, how he lost his twin and his pa, how even I don't really belong to him.

A second later, the driver is back carrying a lunch pail. A man in a cap stops him on the street and goes on and on about Franklin D. Roosevelt, who people say will be the next President.

Saliva drips down Pa's chin, but I don't wipe it for fear of waking him. Once I saw a rabid dog. It was foaming at the mouth and wildly moving its head about.

It was like someone was yelling in its ears and it was trying to shake off the sound. I wasn't sure what I should do. Pa and Ma were inside a store. The dog was between them and me. But my body knew. My feet were already stepping backward, slowly, toward the car. I reached behind me and opened the door, then climbed in.

Actions are strange that way. Like the day I climbed up on the wall, without really thinking about it, and performed for the kids at school, and made friends with Macon and Gus and Sara. That phrase about the left hand not knowing what the right hand is doing refers to giving charity. But it reminds me of how I feel when I take an action. It's like something within me moves without another part knowing it. Maybe that's how it was with Rhett, when he left us and took Theodore, as far away as Seattle. Maybe it was something Rhett just had to do.

The driver's friend tips his hat and walks away. The driver gets into the cab and turns on the engine. I wait until I hear the door slam and the engine groan. Then quickly and quietly, I slip off the truck onto the street. The truck bed clatters loosely on its wheels as it pulls away. It looks like it could just tumble free at any time. But it won't, I know. It will hold fast and stubborn, like life itself.

30

THOU SHALT NOT STEAL.

—The seventh commandment

Snake Lady said that if people die suddenly, their souls stay trapped on earth. Their voices escape from them and they lose their light. So they move only as shadows and can't warn us about danger or the mistakes we might make.

All they can do is watch. In that way, they are like God.

She was nice, Snake Lady. I miss her. People have been kind to me. Strangers have seemed to love me more than my own parents. I try to imagine where she is now, as I keep my tired legs moving past apartment buildings, with their laundry lines covered in clothes like flags, to the busier district where there are shops. It's been ages since I have eaten or drunk.

In the cool garden of Gethsemane, at a Passover Seder, beneath swaying olive trees and a sky the color of blackbird wings, Jesus created a new commandment. Betrayal by Judas, desertion by those he trusted, humiliation, torture, and death were quickly to come his way, but like any good teacher, Jesus wanted to give just one more lesson.

"Where I am going, you cannot come," Jesus said. "I give you a new commandment, that you love one another. By this you will know that you are my disciples, if you have love for one another."

Simple enough. At least for me. And this is what I tell myself, that the one commandment, Jesus' last, replaces all the rest.

The streets are busy, but people don't seemed rushed. Maybe it's Saturday. Couples walk arm in arm. A child carries an ice cream cone, and if her mother wasn't nearby, I just might snatch it from her; that is how parched I feel. Thou shalt not covet thy neighbor's ice cream.

Bleeker's Bakery and Grocer is the most crowded shop on the street. I go in. There are beautiful pastries, meats, salads behind a glass case, and rolls and doughnuts on a counter. It's hard to imagine that anyone could be hungry in the world, with so much in just one shop. I hear my heart beating as I open an ice-box and pull out a bottle of ginger ale, grab a roll, and back slowly toward the door.

"Hey!" I hear a voice. Something brushes against my hair, reaches for me. The bell on the door jangles like nerves. I run out as fast as my legs will carry me, knocking into a boy on a tricycle and a woman with a dog, until I get to a small square with a bench and a row of bushes. I duck under the bushes. I watch for the shopkeeper, a policeman, whoever is after me, but then I realize, no one is.

Leaving the bottle in the bushes, I step out into the heat. A woman makes a sour face. I must look quite a sight. A blind man fumbles on the street and no one clears a path for him. Another man whistles at a woman in a polka-dot dress. A boy hawks newspapers at a corner. I peer at the date. August 22. There is a story about a man dying of exhaustion at a dance marathon, and one about a family who snuck into someone's barn to drink the milk from their cows.

"Move on," the paperboy says. "You can pay if you want the news."

"Which way to St. Andrews?" I ask, more angrily than I intended. If he wants me to move, he can answer me.

I am firmly planted on earth now—no more walking on air. I need to do battle like the rest of them.

31

WHEN GOD CLOSES A DOOR, HE OPENS A WINDOW.

—*Old saying*

After walking for what seems like hours, I come upon the dirt road lined with poplars, their leaves spinning in the breeze like green coins.

The air seems instantly cooler and my heart opens as the small convent appears. There is nobody in the reception room, so I wander down the hall until I hear Ma's familiar cough.

Ma is in a room all by herself. Her bed is in the center of the room. There is a little table next to it and a chair in the corner. On the wall is a cross with a crucified Jesus.

Ma is reading the Bible. It is the first time I've seen

her smile since Michigan, when the small ruffled shoots of our carrots peered up out of the ground, when she watched the Easter play with Rhett.

"June!" She reaches out for me. My heart feels fit to burst at seeing Ma again, knowing how close I came to being taken away. "I was just remembering when you and I made biscuits that snowy day in Michigan. We ate them all up with maple syrup."

"How do you feel, Ma?"

"The sisters are treating me very well here. The bed is such a comfort. And I got lunch on a tray. It's like being a little girl again. How are you? Have you had something to eat today?"

"I had a roll."

"Where's your pa?"

"He's looking for work in town," I say, surprised how easily the lie rolls off my tongue. "Men aren't allowed to come in here. Remember?"

"Yes, that's right, except the priests and doctors. I was reading Song of Solomon. They say that Song of Solomon, Proverbs, and Ecclesiastes were all written by Solomon. But I don't see it. How could anyone who wrote something as generous as Song of Solomon write something as stingy as Proverbs? Maybe Ecclesiastes . . . after he was old and felt disappointed by life."

I sit in the chair. The walk here has taken me two hours. It will be dark before I get back to town. I don't exactly feel like discussing scripture.

"Do you and your pa have someplace to stay?" she asks.

"Uh . . . yes."

"He always finds something, that man. He's the most resourceful person I ever met. I remember when we first set off together and he had spent every dime on that suitcase. He walked right up to the conductor and told him that letting us on the train would save his soul. He talked and talked until the conductor got so flustered, he not only let us on, but gave us lunch, too."

"Can I have the rest of that?" I point to a tray with a bit of leftover egg.

"Oh, you mustn't, because I'm contagious. In fact, this ward is quarantined. I'm surprised they let you come in here at all."

"I just walked in. I didn't ask."

"I wish you could stay with me here, where you'd be well taken care of."

I lean back in the chair. On one corner of the ceiling there is a painting of a plump gold angel. It seems out of place in the stark room. The angel's face is round, its cheeks pink. The angel is well taken care of, that's for sure. And suddenly Ma, the angel, even Jesus resting on the cross, a roof over his head, make me feel mad. "Ma. Remember what you told me in Hooverville?"

"Now, June, I regret that very much. I thought I was dying and I had some impulse to . . ." She tosses the Bible onto her lap. "Well, your parent is the person who's raised you, plain and simple."

"So what happened to this man, my . . . father?"

"I told him about you. I told him that our one rash act had resulted in a child. Well, you'da had to see his face. His whole life he'd thought of nothing but escaping Providence. He wanted to go to law school and then become a politician. That spring he was accepted to Harvard. Best college in the country. We were so excited. We celebrated. Ha! You were the result of that celebration."

"And?"

"He should've spoken up for my hand then, asked me to marry him. Instead, he told me that he couldn't let a child interfere with his future. He said that if he had to stay and work in his parents' business, support a family, he'd die. He'd just die. . . ."

"Then what?"

"That's all. He abandoned me. Us. I'll never forgive him."

"Do you know where he is?"

Ma closes her eyes.

"Questions sure do make you sleepy, Ma. Last time I was asking you about this, you were tired too."

"Why, June?" She opens her eyes. "Since when do you talk to me like that?"

"Where is he?"

"I don't know right now."

"I want to write to Rhett. You must know where *he* is."

"He went off to Seattle with that boy. I think part of the problem with your pa and me has been having Rhett always trailing around with us. It didn't really give your pa a chance to stand on his own feet."

"You must have an address for him!"

"I don't," she says.

I walk over to Ma's suitcase and open it up.

"June, whatever are you doing?"

I rifle through her things like a robber. There's two patched worn dresses, an old sachet that smells like mothballs, a scarf, and a sweater. In the torn lining of the suitcase is a small scrap of paper with three addresses written on it. All of them are in Rhode Island.

"Which one is for his ma?"

"None of your business. You'd think I'd have thrown that paper away," Ma says. "I have those addresses memorized backward and forward."

"I'll write to all three of them," I say.

"I just might become a Catholic." Ma emphasizes every syllable of the word so that Cath-o-lic sounds like some kind of sucking candy rather than a big religion. "The sisters live here in peace and quiet and prayer. They serve others. Most of *them* have vows of silence."

"Like Rhett."

"Yes."

"Is Rhett my father?"

Ma's eyes move to the crucified Jesus. I remember something from when I was young. We were visiting someone in a hospital once and Ma told Pa, "We're all Jesus and Jesus is us."

"Like that's some kind of *news*," Pa had sneered.

"I mean . . . we all suffer the same way He did, so why don't *we* redeem anyone, least of all ourselves?"

A discussion followed then, because I asked about the word *redeemed*, and Pa said it was what happened when you took your bottle back to the store and they gave you half a cent.

"Are you going to answer me?" I say.

"No."

"No, you're not going to answer, or no, he's not my pa?"

"Your pa is your pa. The one who raised you. The one who made sure you were fed and clothed and who taught you to walk on that tightrope so you'd be special and know excellence. The one who has *always* been by your side. Not someone who comes and goes as he pleases. That's all there is to the story. That's all I'm going to say."

I look at Ma, all safe and snug in her bed, not knowing that I have nowhere to go, no food, no money, no pa. She doesn't know anything. And maybe she doesn't want to.

32

TO DO JUSTICE, AND TO LOVE GOODNESS,
AND TO WALK MODESTLY WITH YOUR GOD.

—*MICAH*

Aside from being patient, keeping their mouths shut, and doing what they're told, the other quality for which girls are rewarded in fairy tales is long flowing hair, preferably gold.

My hair is gold, when it's clean, and flows down to my waist. It is the first thing to go at the orphanage.

The Sweet Home Orphanage for Girls rises out of the "red-light district," in what used to be a "respectable" neighborhood. Miss Price, who is in charge of it, tells me that the orphanage itself was once a church. The surrounding buildings housed families, bakeries, butchers, and barbers. Now they house pool halls, speakeasies, and "houses of ill repute." Miss Price has told me, "Never leave the orphanage without me, or you may end up in one of them houses of ill repute."

Miss Price is a tall lady. She stands very straight. It's like there is an ironing board stuck into the back of her dress.

She was sympathetic when I told her about being deserted by my parents. She clicked her tongue and said that under the rules, they had to be dead for me to seek shelter, but that we could fudge a little while she tries to find them.

I'm interested in the idea of being an orphan. An orphan can choose her own course. I once saw a boat set loose from its mooring. It was on a river in Ohio. A fire erupted; the dock glowed black and red. You could see every particle of the wood, like grains of sand, before it tumbled piecemeal into the river.

The rope holding the small dinghy burned through and the boat was let loose. It turned and bobbed softly, like a hand waving good-bye, before it floated into the river.

Of course, I'm not really an orphan. Ma is just an hour's walk away. But no one knows this. I have to be sneaky to get out to visit her, my sins multiplying by the second.

I had walked the city looking for shelter until a policeman, eyeing my torn filthy clothes, brought me here.

Miss Price is very big on cleanliness. *Cleanliness is next to godliness,* she said that first night, as she scrubbed my nails with a brush and bathed me in freezing water. "It's the lice," Miss Price said as her scissors snipped away my hair. "Once they come, we'll never get them out."

She thought I was crying about my hair, but I wasn't. Tears came to my eyes because I remembered when I was very little and Ma combed and curled my hair and put it up into bows. I remembered Sara grabbing my hand every day so we could walk home together, and Gus socking me, and Rhett putting his arm around me.

Miss Price's hands were rough, but they were hands.

"This is probably the only orphanage in the world where you get to take ballet," she said. "Madame Gold gives lessons here for free twice a week. She gives them out of charity because she was an orphan too. You will enjoy ballet," she commanded, scrubbing at my neck with a bristle brush.

Miss Price isn't a bad sort, but the girls here are

pretty mean. Since I'm new, I have to clean out the fireplaces and toilets. My first day, the biggest girl, Ada, tried to shove my head into the toilet. She said she didn't like my looks.

Luckily, she slipped on the soapy floor and I got away. *God works in mysterious ways,* Ma says.

Most of our time is spent on what Miss Price calls "upkeep." Since it used to be a church, the orphanage has a bell tower, tall windows, and a staircase that is about as cold as anywhere I've ever been, and darker than the inside of a whale's belly.

From the windows, you can look down at life on the street. Vendors hawk their wares. Musicians practice their saxophones and clarinets. There are men who sell women, and the women who are sold, wearing clothes bright with sin: red silk, purple lace, black feathers.

In the evenings the customers come: men looking for company, couples in evening clothes who are "slumming" or wanting to hear the new music, jazz, which the girls here call "black music." The women who step out of these cars have long evening gowns and shoes so beautiful, their feet don't seem to touch the ground.

The orphans pretend they are the well-dressed ladies—wear socks on their hands like gloves, sway their hips when they walk, practice kissing on their wrists, practice other things with pillows.

At night, Miss Price closes all the windows and draws the heavy curtains. Even so, the music leaks in through the cracks, a temptation that leaves us restless, our feet and hands tapping.

The girls tell me that the orphanage is haunted, that the priest who once held services here hung himself above the pulpit one Sunday morning just before the congregation entered. He had fallen in love, but since priests can't marry, he couldn't do anything about it.

I don't get the sense of any ghosts, except when I walk up those cold, dark stairs and feel like someone is watching me, someone who may or may not be swinging above the pulpit.

I doubt that Pa would approve of ballet, but it is the best part about being here. Because of my work on the tightrope, it comes very easily to me. I can plié, leap, and pirouette with ease. My balance is perfect. Ada usually cuts ballet. But when she does come, she dances angrily. It's as if she is at war with the air. She doesn't *tendu* or *frappé,* she kicks. She doesn't port de bras, she punches.

One of the girls tells me that Ada's dad tried to turn her into his wife. Another says that Ada murdered both of her parents by setting the house on fire.

Even though Miss Price chases Ada with a wash-cloth constantly, she is always dirty. I sometimes think she rubs coal on herself just to peeve Miss Price. She has great big legs and a tall thin torso. It's like someone put a hippo bottom with a giraffe top.

One day, Ada shoves me against the wall: "Do you have a boyfriend, ballerina?"

"No."

"Have you ever even been kissed?"

"Uh-uh," I answer. I figure Fish Man doesn't count since I didn't want him to.

"I can find a boy who'll kiss you. There's one who comes on the weekends to fix things and he kisses any-body who wants to be kissed, and more. His name is Roger. One of his ears was bit off by a dog. He'll put his thing in you."

"That's okay."

"Don't tell me that's not why you sneak out." She twists my arm behind my back.

I don't say anything. I have a feeling I'm better off having Ada think I'm meeting a boy than my ma.

Two girls, Kate and Lisa, come by then. "Let her go," Kate says, but it doesn't sound like she really means it.

"Break her arm," Lisa commands.

"I just might." Ada twists harder.

"Let go," I beg.

"Too bad you had to cut your hair," Ada says. "It sure was pretty."

I swing my leg and kick her. She winces but doesn't let go.

"Here comes Miss Price," Kate whispers.

Ada lets go. She and Lisa dash off, laughing.

"Miss Price isn't really coming," Kate says.

"Oh. Thanks."

"You got to whip her," Kate says.

"Ada?"

"Yeah. It's the only way she'll stop."

33

NO WAY OF ESCAPE IS IN SIGHT,
NO ONE COMES TO RESCUE ME.

—PSALM 142

There's not a lot in the Bible about people's hair, but one person has real problems when he loses his. Samson's long hair gives him exceptional strength. He can kill thirty men at once. No one can beat him, until he gives the secret of his strength away to his girl-friend, Delilah. While he sleeps, she has his hair cut off. His power diminished, the Philistines capture him, gouge out his eyes, and parade him in front of a jeering crowd.

The fact that I am Miss Price's favorite doesn't make my life any easier. Most of the girls side with Ada in calling out insults to me, although it is only Ada who twists my arm or kicks me. I try to stay close to Miss Price when I can, to avoid Ada's attention. I do extra chores, offer to help her carry groceries, and wash clothes. "You're a good girl," Miss Price has said. It made me feel bad that I stole a dime from her to post letters to Rhett.

Kate is not a good girl, but she is my only friend. At night, she sneaks out and goes to the speakeasy, where men give her things: a beaded purse, a glove, a lipstick. She wants me to go with her, and maybe some night, I will.

"Do you know why the old hag is called Miss Price?" Kate whispers one day when we're at mass.

"No."

"Because she has a price. Anyone can buy her off. Think about that next time you want to sneak away to see your boyfriend."

"I don't have a boyfriend," I insist, but I do think hard about that, since it has been two weeks since I've last seen Ma. Both times I tried to leave, Miss Price caught me.

My next chance doesn't come until Saturday, when Miss Price goes shopping and Father Chris comes to give us lessons. He wears a long black dress, like the nuns, but he never talks much about God. Instead, he goes on about nouns and predicates, the "dissection" of words into manageable syllables that can be accepted into our impoverished brains, like little pieces of bread for birds.

As he leaves, I chase after him. "Father!"

"What is it, child? You're supposed to be inside."

"If a descriptive word modifies a verb rather than a noun, then what happens?"

"What happens?"

"Yes."

"It's an adverb."

"But what if it's a complicated sentence and the descriptive word applies to the noun *and* the verb?"

"Now now, my girl. Sister Maria has died. I must make a call at the convent." He goes to his horse and pats it, then climbs onto the wagon.

"Why don't you ever talk about God?"

Father Chris clicks his tongue and grabs the reins; he pauses. "It's impractical," he says. "A bunch of orphans need to learn some skills."

"But you're a priest. . . ."

"I was brought up in a very good family. There was time for such things."

"You mean there's no time for God if you're poor?"

"You know the difference between us and God? God doesn't want. I don't mean He's not hungry or tired. I mean He doesn't *want*. He doesn't desire. And that makes all the difference because without desire, there is no greed, no jealousy, no evil. There's only goodness."

"That's the only difference?"

"God is impossible to comprehend. But grammar— that's something of which you can be sure." He shakes the reins. I duck behind and climb onto the back of the wagon. I'm getting good at climbing on and off of things.

It is only when we've started moving that I think about what the priest said. Does he mean that God is only for the rich, for those who have "time for such things"? It reminds me of Pa's father, who thought that only certain people were elected to go to heaven. Who wants to be a part of a God who gives special treatment only to some? It doesn't seem fair.

The cart hits a rut and I am almost thrown off. We pass the diner with the fish sign. Only now the diner is boarded up. Where it used to say FRIED FISH AND HASH BROWNS, the sign says THE FUTURE IS HERE.

I try to imagine a future for this country ten, twenty,

thirty, forty years from now. Will there still be cars? Will folks pass the time sitting around the radio? Will there still be so many hungry living in cardboard houses and tin sheds? Will the string of the world have snapped, like Ma once said, or will it still be holding tight?

What good is the future if things don't get better?

When the horses slow to turn onto the poplar-lined road, I jump off the wagon. I wait a bit until I'm sure Father Chris is inside.

This time, though, I am stopped as I try to sneak through the hall to Ma's room. The nun peers at me over her spectacles. "Who are you?" she asks. "This area is quarantined."

"I'm here to see my ma."

"Who?"

"Agnes Dial."

"She has left us. Don't be frightened. I don't mean she has passed on. Her health improved. It was just bronchitis, after all. We needed the bed."

"When?"

"Last week," the old nun says.

"Where did she go?"

"We never ask those questions, dear. Just be thankful that she is well."

34

MY OWN ARM BROUGHT ME VICTORY.

—*ISAIAH*

Ada has my hair. She is holding it up around her face, attempting a pirouette, to the cheers of the other girls. "I'm ballerina June, the high and mighty," she chants, leaping over a chair and knocking it down.

The thought that has been floating in my head finally surfaces, that the lie I've told has turned into truth, that I am now an orphan.

Twice I have been to the convent, but there has been no word of my mother. I have received several different stories from the nuns. Ma went home to Providence. She went to join my father in Los Angeles. She disappeared.

I think about Hagar being cast into the desert by Sarah with her son, Ishmael; her grief that Ishmael might die of thirst; her willingness to stay with him. I try to imagine all the mothers in the Bible, but I can't think of any who abandon their children.

"Here's your hair, ballerina, scattering in the wind."

I'm amazed at how well my hair has been preserved: the color, the shape, the curl is all the same as when it was on my head weeks ago. Small pieces drop to the floor as Ada dances. Clumps become feathers, then wisps.

The girls circle us, cheering. Even Kate joins in the chant: *Fight, fight, fight.*

People have done worse things than abandon their children. In the Bible, at the end of Judges, a man shoves his wife out the door to be raped by the townspeople. He does this because they had asked for *him*. The Bible never mentions this man's name and I certainly don't need to know it. But because of the woman's rape and death, a war begins. Many people die.

The floor is covered in my hair now. It would have been nice to have it, actually, to have tied it in a ribbon and given it to Ma to remember. When I see her again. If I see her again.

She could have waited there. She could've waited for me at the convent. She could have tried harder to find me.

"Cat got your tongue?" Ada kicks me. My knee buckles from the strike.

Something in me shifts. The whole country is waiting for poverty to end. But does anything ever happen? The way I feel is the same way I felt when I jumped off the truck. Like there was two of me, a body and a mind, the body taking over from the mind, like it wasn't going to wait anymore.

Ada doesn't notice me until I am on the bed. But by then it is too late. Like a diver off a high cliff, I leap at her, carry her to the ground with me, speed my fists at her face like spinning wheels. Her blood is warm. Her body is soft, her bones small and sharp.

Words pour from my mouth with each strike and I actually have to listen to know what I'm saying. "Come back. Come back. Come back."

"June!" Miss Price shrieks.

Ada's hands come up to mine.

"Whatever are you doing?" Miss Price yanks me off of Ada. "There's blood all over the floor."

"I'm sorry," I mumble. What else can I say?

"I honestly can't believe this. The two of you. Like animals."

"She started it." Lisa points at me, then the others join in. *She started it. She started it.*

"A man is here to see you, June," Miss Price says. "Go and wash yourself up immediately!"

"Good one, ballerina," Ada whispers. "Didn't think you had it in you."

EVEN WHEN THE GATES OF HEAVEN ARE
CLOSED TO PRAYER THEY ARE OPEN TO TEARS.
—*The Talmud*

Miss Price shoves my whole head into the washtub. For a minute it seems like she will never let me up. It makes me think of Pa's drowned twin, my uncle, who I never got to meet.

Pa didn't have any money when my grandpa left him in Florida. All he had was his tent, his clothes, and the hat in which he collected money for God. That very evening he took his hat and went to the construction site of the hotel. The men were drinking. It was the end of their day.

Pa told some jokes to the men to get their attention, and then he talked about Mary Magdalene, her sinfulness, her love of Christ, so intense it was almost romantic. He knew all these men building by themselves in the marshes would listen harder if he talked about a woman.

Times were better then. One of the men offered him a share of supper. He said Pa's preaching reminded him of his church back home, eased his homesickness. A couple of others dropped some coins into his hat. His life as a preacher began.

The water makes me shiver as it flows down my face and neck, my arms. My knuckles ache from the contact with Ada. Miss Price gives me a clean skirt and blouse.

I take my time dressing. I don't want to make Pa wait, but I want to look decent. I wonder just how mad he is going to be at me for deserting him. I say my first prayer to God in many weeks. "Please, let Ma be there too."

And if she's not? The thought makes me shudder, but I won't let it in. Life just *isn't* without Ma. It can't be.

There are three clocks in the hall, all telling different times. A cold breeze sweeps across the room from nowhere, reminding me of the heartbroken priest who hung himself. The heart *can* be broken. I know that now. I should have known it all along.

I open the door.

The first thing I see is his back as he stands looking out the window. He is dressed in a tweed suit and
broad-rimmed hat. He must've done well in
California. He looks bigger somehow, as if he's eaten
lots of meals. Ma is nowhere to be seen.

"Pa?"

He turns slowly, his eyes taking me in—my thin-
ness, my short hair—and I realize my mistake.

It is Rhett. Cleaner and better dressed than the
last time I saw him, but Rhett.

"June?" His voice comes out sounding different
than the mumble of his dreams. It comes out low and
smooth. "It took a while for me to get your letter."

He speaks! I want to run to him, but his rich
clothes and his *voice* make me feel suddenly shy.

"This is your father?" Miss Price asks, looking
from one of us to the other.

I have seen Miss Price turn people away who have
come to claim girls: aunts, uncles, friends of the family.

"I am her father," he says, in a voice so sure that
the words can only be true.

I don't know if it's the pain in my legs from where
Ada kicked me, or the chill I feel, or the weight of
Rhett's voice, the words like a thunderstorm after a
long drought, but my knees buckle and I fall in a heap

on the floor. Rhett rushes over. He gathers me up like a bundle of firewood.

Miss Price waits a second, then she comes over and tugs at me. "Do you think, sir, that you can just desert a child and expect to pick her up at the drop of a hat without any repercussions?"

"I will certainly compensate you for June's time here." Rhett pulls out his wallet. "I . . . we didn't know she was here. She disappeared."

Miss Price frowns. "There's much I didn't know about June myself. Now that I look at you both, I do see the resemblance."

"Will you accept? . . ." Rhett holds out money.

I remember Kate's gibe about Miss Price having a price.

"If this is a donation, I could use it . . . to make new dresses for the girls." She takes the money.

"Yes, certainly. A donation."

"June, you may get your things."

I haven't got any things, so I just leave the room and stand outside the door a minute and try to catch my breath, Rhett's words ringing in my ears: *I am her father, her father, her father.*

36

WHERE YOU GO, I WILL GO. WHERE YOU LIE DOWN,
SO WILL I. YOUR PEOPLE WILL BE MY PEOPLE;
YOUR GOD WILL BE MY GOD.

—*BOOK OF RUTH*

There's an old story that I've always liked about a man whose town has flooded. His neighbors offer to help him get away, but he refuses to leave. "God will take care of me," the man says faithfully.

The flood gets worse. The water rises. Another neighbor comes in a boat and offers the man a ride. But the man refuses to go. "God will take care of me."

The water rises higher. The man climbs onto the roof. Now a policeman arrives. "This is the last boat," the policeman says. "Get in and I'll save you."

"God will save me."

The policeman rushes away. The water rises. The man drowns.

When the man gets to heaven he upbraids God. "How could you do this to me? I had faith in you and you let me drown."

"I sent you your neighbors and two boats," God says. "What more do you expect?"

As we walk to the car, Rhett holds my arm. It's almost like he knows how wobbly I feel. His words come slowly, as if he's still out of practice. "I'm sorry. This is all a shock. It just . . ."

"Are you . . ."

"I couldn't go on anymore, just following along and trying to make sure things went right for you."

Behind me, the orphanage is already shrinking. I can imagine Ada surrounded by the other girls, examining her bruises and cuts in the broken bathroom mirror. She will be enjoying the attention. That is what she needs.

It is early. The streets are empty and I'm glad that Rhett won't see the fancy ladies, the mean-faced men. The sinful sleep late. Rhett won't know that the large stain on the sidewalk is from a woman whose "boyfriend" slit her throat when she tried to run off, and that nobody answered her cries for help. He won't know what I know.

I want to ask him about Ma, but my tongue feels as thick in my mouth as the day I had to say good-bye to Miss O'Doul.

Rhett stops in front of a car. And then I see him right there in front of me, a freckle-faced miracle in tweed knickers.

"Theodore!"

"June!"

I hug him so tightly, he practically gasps for air.

"What happened to your beautiful hair?"

"They chopped it off, and there's a girl there who stole it and I got in a fight with her."

"You fought?"

"It's a long story." I glance at Rhett. I don't want to tell it in front of him.

"This is our car," Theodore says. "It's a La Salle."

Sometimes, in fairy tales, things like this happen. A girl may be poor and downtrodden, her hair chopped off, her hopes defeated—then magic occurs and a pumpkin turns into a carriage, the rags she wears into beautiful clothes.

"Better get in," Rhett urges. It's like he's afraid

Miss Price will change her mind and come running after us.

"Is this your aunt's?" I ask Theodore.

"It's mine and Rhett's," he answers proudly. "And we have a store in Providence."

"Didn't you go to Seattle?"

"We did, but we never found my aunt. We went to her house and it wasn't there anymore. Then we went all over asking about her. No one knew anything. I'd only met her once. She visited when I was seven and I remember she didn't seem to like me. She kept telling me to go out and play so she could talk to my mom."

"We." He keeps saying it. Who is *my* "we"?

"Sit back, Theo," Rhett instructs. The car pulls away from the curb, from the street, the block, the city of Dayton, Ohio, the orphanage.

The day is the color of pencil lead. Fields of corn sprawl out as far as I can see. The corn has been picked long ago, eaten with butter and salt at long wooden tables, eaten in the grass by picnicking families.

"Where's Ma?" I finally ask.

"She's in California now," Rhett says. "Los Angeles. But they're getting ready to go to Nevada. They're just waiting for you to come on the train."

"Ma left me here," I say.

"Well, young lady," Rhett scolds like a father, "you didn't exactly tell her where you were. She thought you were with Alfred and when she was released from the convent and couldn't reach anyone, she went to find Aimee McPherson at Angelus Temple."

"Was he there?"

Rhett nods.

"Preaching?"

"Cleaning," Theodore answers for him. "He's the janitor. He's even getting paid. And he was given a room to live in and everything."

"Did you see them?" I ask Theodore. The whole world's just been turning away while I've been sitting in the same place.

"Uh-huh."

"They won't stay in Nevada for long," Rhett says. "They plan to keep heading north toward Alaska."

"Are you coming too?" I ask. "Are you both coming on the train?"

Rhett coughs and clears his throat. "Theodore and I are going to live in Rhode Island. I'm not going to be following them anymore. I have to attend to my mother's affairs now that she's getting on in years...."

His *mother*? Is she then my grandma?

"And Theodore needs a place to settle down," he says.

"Oh." A line comes to my mind from one of the psalms: *My heart is like wax. It is melted within my breast.*

The car is moving, but somehow I feel absolutely still, like I'm suspended on the tightrope above the earth, and can never ever come down.

"You didn't tell her what her mother said," Theo whispers to Rhett.

"What?" I ask.

"You got to tell her!"

Rhett pulls the car over to the side of the road by the endless dead fields, the graveyards for corn. He turns around and looks me in the eye, his eyes like mine, green flecks floating around in blue.

"Your ma said that you get to choose," he says, his voice choked, almost scared.

"I get to choose?"

"Yes." Rhett looks out the window.

"Choose *what*?"

"Whether to go with them or come with us!" Theodore answers.

"I get to choose?"

Rhett looks back at me. "That's what your ma said."

37

WE WERE LIKE THOSE WHO DREAM.

—*PSALM 126*

The town of Providence was established in the 1630s when a man named Roger Williams was banished from Massachusetts for his religious beliefs. Like Pa, he was a minister, but he believed that everyone should be free to practice in their own way.

Other people seeking the freedom to worship God soon flocked to the area. Eventually, the state of Rhode Island—and Providence Plantations—became a place where Jews, Catholics, Baptists, Quakers, Unitarians, and even atheists came to live together peacefully.

In the dictionary, the word *Providence* means the

foreseeing care and guidance of God over all the world's creatures. I know because I read this. My grandma has three dictionaries, and books and books, on the shelves of her library.

When I first walked into Rhett's ma's house, she was baking a cake. She took one look at me and dropped the cup of flour in her hands. "My girl!" She rushed over and put her big arms around me. When she finally stood back and looked at me, we all laughed because my hair and face were covered in flour.

"What about me?" Theo begged, and Grandma pulled him over. For a while she just stood there blinking at both of us, like we were angels fresh from heaven.

Rhett had never told his mother about me until he came back with Theodore from Seattle. That was when he decided that his way of making amends to me and Ma wasn't working. Times were too hard to be dragging through the country, especially when his ma needed him here to run the store and help with the factory, and Theo needed to settle down and study. How else would he ever get to be president?

That first afternoon, my grandma laid out a meal on the table like I'd never seen: roasted chicken and stuffing, carrots, turnips, cranberries, corn bread, and salad made with apples and nuts.

"Is it a holiday?" I asked.

Theodore laughed. "We always eat this way here."

I couldn't help wishing that Ma and Pa were there too, to eat, and maybe even enjoy themselves. I wished everyone was there from Hooverville to feel full once again.

"June," Theodore whispered when I sat next to him, "I guess we won't get to be married now, 'cause we're brother and sister."

"I guess not." But that was okay with me, because I'd rather have a brother anyway, and it's probably better that he's not my twin.

After we ate, my grandma and Rhett took me into their store, where folks can buy dry goods, jarred fruits and preserves, hair ribbons, cloth, and hog feed.

"This is all yours?" I asked my grandma.

She smiled. She does that a lot. "Ours," she said.

38

THIS AT LAST IS BONE OF MY BONES
AND FLESH OF MY FLESH.

— *GENESIS*

Lately, at odd times, I think about my ma. Like when little girls come into our shop for fabric, thread, and buttons. I think about how much Ma liked being a child here, and looking out her window at the New England seasons. Or like when Theodore and I are in class writing sums, and I remember how much she loved school.

For a while, I felt hurt that she didn't care whether I joined her and Pa. I thought maybe she was glad to be rid of me. But then, one Saturday afternoon, when the shop was empty and I'd just had a big lunch, I fell asleep against a sack of flour and had that familiar dream. I was a preacher dressed in white, like Aimee

Semple McPherson. And I was standing in a church before a group of seekers, afraid I wouldn't know what to say. But this time, when I opened my mouth, the story came out about Solomon and the two mothers, the false one and the true. How when Solomon says he will cut the baby in two, the real mother gives him up.

She gives him up because she loves him.

I got a letter from Ma a few weeks back. She said they were in Arizona, where the sand is white as snow and so hot that the creatures that inhabit it come out only at night. She said the air is dry and easy to breathe.

What she didn't say is how she explained me staying in Rhode Island to Pa, or whether she told him that I don't belong to him. I wonder how he feels having to summon all those tired souls without me there to entertain them.

I wonder if he misses me.

One night, when I was little, Pa promised that if I could do a flip on the rope the first try he would give me a prize. We were in Missouri. The air was like wet gauze. The moon was full. Frogs were croaking by the river. I got right up and performed a perfect flip.

He looked perplexed. I don't think he actually had a prize. "What do you want, June?" he said.

"To stay up tonight," I said.

"All right," he agreed, and the two of us walked down to the river. We sat on the bank, watching the strange ballooning of the frogs' throats as they croaked, listening to their lonely calls. It was so warm Pa let me put my feet into the water. A fish swam past, touched my ankle. I didn't mind.

Here, it is cold. The Indians have ridden away with their summer. The leaves on the trees are the color of copper and flames. Tomorrow is Halloween, the night of the dead, when children in costumes will race house to house, collecting apples and doughnuts and candy.

Eggs will be thrown against walls, black cats set onto porches to bring bad luck, and bonfires lit in the street.

Hari and Kari said that Halloween was the one day when they could "go as ourselves." They were joking, of course, but I could see what they meant and how their life was different from anyone else's in the world.

Rhett's ma, my grandma, brought four pumpkins over from the garden. Rhett carved a face scary enough to fend off the dead. I tried to carve a face to look like Macon, but it ended up looking like one of Mr. Shepherd's cabbages instead. Grandma carved hers to look like a lady, and she put a hat on it.

"Rhett has changed so much," I say to Theodore

when Rhett helps Grandma carry the pumpkins to the front porch.

"Maybe he's just gone back to who he was before," Theodore says.

"Maybe."

Pa's idea was that a photograph steals your soul, but maybe that also happens when your voice, like a trapped bird, is caged. Even if it is your own choice.

My grandma is rushing to finish our costumes. Theodore is going as Abraham Lincoln. She made him a tall hat out of black paper and drew a beard on his face with charcoal. I'm going as a witch.

Pa always said Halloween was a pagan holiday. It was a sin to even mention it. He would never let me carve pumpkins and dress up, would not allow me to attend the bonfire with the other kids, or run through the streets after dark.

But I can find God in things he never dreamed of. I can find God in my grandma's smile or in Rhett's voice. I can find God in the round golden pumpkins, the cold velvety night, the red apples, the goblins and witches clamoring down the street banging pots and pans.

I can find God in the white moon, the howls and laughter and shouts, even in the tree branches swaying in the wind, shaking their leaves like the black arms of ghosts.